Death Signs

Also by H. Edward Hunsburger

Crossfire

Death Signs

H. Edward Hunsburger

Walker and Company
New York

First published in the United States of America in 1987 by the Walker Publishing Company, Inc.

Published simultaneously in Canada by Thomas Allen & Son Canada, Limited, Markham, Ontario

Library of Congress Cataloging-in-Publication Data

Hunsburger, H. Edward.
    Death signs.

    I. Title.
PS3558.U4673D4 1987   813′.54   87-10405
ISBN 0-8027-5679-4

Printed in the United States of America

10 9 8 7 6 5 4 3 2 1

For Christine, who already knows all the reasons why.

1

As the flickering yellow light changed suddenly to red, Mattie tapped the brakes, swore and then hit them hard, bringing the Mustang to a screaming halt in the middle of the white-lined pedestrian crossing.

Her hands were shaking. In spite of the cold, her palms were slick with sweat. She slowly loosened her grip on the steering wheel, took a deep breath, closed her eyes for a second and then forced them open again. In the post rush hour quiet the intersection was deserted, with depthless shadows and dark store fronts, and the distant pink haze of a pizzeria sign in the next block. No people. Not a single one in sight. The only real noise was her convertible idling, sounding as though it were made entirely of spare parts, none of which were ever intended to fit together. She could feel the car's jerky vibration through the tape-patched seat and all along her spine. She thought she could smell something too. A faint odor of burning oil or rubber? Something disastrous and pyrotechnical just waiting to happen. Something ticking the time away like an impatient terrorist's bomb.

Shaking her head, Mattie forced a smile. Imagining the worst wasn't helping anything. She'd had one of those days. The kind that no one, least of all your mother, ever warns you about. It had started out with a confrontation with Gus Kellerman, God's gift to public education, then moved quickly along to a missed luncheon appointment she'd been looking forward to all month long. Finally the day had ended with a badly botched parent-teacher conference. She still wasn't sure whose fault *that* was. But since she'd avoided even thinking about it, it was probably hers.

Waiting out the eternal red, Mattie drummed her fingers against the steering wheel and shifted her knees a little to get them closer to the tepid flow of air from the Mustang's heater. She wondered if today was just a one-shot deal or, worse still, only the beginning of a long string of small, personal misfortunes. She'd never believed in reincarnation or anything like that. But at least it was some kind of explanation.

Friday, October 17th. It could be a judgment, a long postponed reckoning for dark and deadly deeds committed in a previous lifetime. Maybe someone up there had given the cosmic Wheel of Fortune a hard, wild spin and come up with Mattie Ann Shayne. Today. This lifetime. Retroactive retribution for *all* previous sins. Mattie stared out at the darkness and grinned. Had she lived other lives? Had she really been that bad? Not that she'd been a complete living saint in this lifetime. But a day like today she just didn't deserve.

Up ahead the light changed back to green. Behind her a car horn began to bleat insistently. Muttering to herself, Mattie shifted gears and gave it the gas. The Mustang responded sluggishly, finally lurching forward like an old tank trying to claw its way up a muddy hillside. Squeezing past her, a new Toyota Supra shot by, its taillights disappearing in a matter of seconds, swallowed up by the murky gray twilight.

It was nearly seven when she finally turned the ailing convertible into her driveway. All the way over from Nicollet the noise under the hood had grown increasingly louder, an ominous rumbling of repair bills yet to come. Letting the engine idle, Mattie leaned forward and pressed an ear against the cold, grainy vinyl of the dash. The noise seemed to have settled into something that was a cross between a squeal and a moan. She was tired, and she knew it was probably just her imagination, but it sounded more than anything as though something small and unpleasant had crawled in there to die.

She cut the engine and slumped back in the seat, suddenly feeling too far gone to move. Through the dirt-speckled windshield she watched as the last, smudged remnants of the setting

2

sun disappeared behind the silver maple in her backyard, smoky streaks of vermilion and gold backlighting the bare gray branches.

Autumn had come early this year, the first cold snap before the end of August. Tonight there was a wind as well. Gusts of it made a dry, snapping sound pushing around the fallen leaves, banking them against the side of the house for a few seconds and then suddenly shifting to whip them back across the scruffy lawn in crazy, gyroscope patterns. And the air that seeped in through the tear in the canvas cartop was laced with a coming frost, so thick, so crystalline pure that Mattie could almost taste it.

Shivering, she grabbed her attaché case and a small, paper sack of groceries, opened the door and swung her long legs out of the car. Something had started to leak in the grocery bag, probably the carton of milk. Mattie shifted her grip, trying to keep the sodden bottom from giving way completely. She could already feel the oozing liquid soaking the front of her trench coat. She slammed the car door shut with her hip and bolted up the graveled drive. The wind stung her face and whipped around her dark blond hair. A sudden icy blast twisted her coattails around her legs, nearly knocking her over.

"Minne*sota*."

Shifting her burdens again, she shouldered open the door to the "three seasons" front porch. What in the world had ever possessed her to move back here? Terminal amnesia? This was the one state in the union that only had *two* seasons—winter and August 17. She dropped her attaché case and then carefully lowered the leaking grocery sack to the floor. Straightening up, she took a slow, calming breath and just stood there for a moment. It had been a hell of a day. But it was over.

As Mattie slipped her key in the lock a glaring yellow-white wash of headlights suddenly flooded the porch. Turning, she heard the crunch of tires on gravel and then the brightness diminished as the car nosed in and came to a smooth stop behind her own. The porch windows were misted from the cold and in the gathering darkness it took her a moment to get a clear fix on the vehicle. It didn't belong to anyone she knew; but there was something uncomfortably familiar about the stark white sedan with its whip antenna and roof-mounted light bar. They had the wrong address. It had to be something like that. After everything that had happened today, what could the cops possibly want with her?

While the engine idled quietly, the door on the driver's side swung open and a young patrolman stepped out. He was tall and rangy, with one of those innocent, open faces that look more at home behind the wheel of a tractor than a big-city patrol car. Holding on to his cap, he dipped his head against the force of the wind and loped up the drive, his heavy black shoes kicking up a spray of gravel behind him.

Mattie swallowed hard and opened the porch door.

"Miss Shayne?"

Mattie nodded. Up close he wasn't as young as she'd first guessed. A webbing of crow's feet tugged at the corners of his pale blue eyes and deep lines bracketed his nose and mouth like cracks in a dry riverbed. That look of innocence was illusionary too. Nothing more than a deception of shadow and fading light.

"Patrolman Tom Detlinger." His fingers brushed the visor of his uniform cap in a casual salute. "We need a sign language interpreter down at County Medical. They just brought in a deaf man—a stabbing victim. There isn't much time."

Nodding again, Mattie turned and yanked her keys out of the door and shoved them in her coat pocket. With a final, fleeting look at her attaché and groceries, she slammed the porch door behind her and ran down the drive.

At least it was warm inside the police cruiser. The interior smelled faintly of gun oil, Old Spice, spilled coffee and stale cigarette smoke. On the front seat a half-eaten hamburger rested on its bright foil wrapping with a little sack of fries propped up next to it. The food was cold enough to have lost whatever aroma it had had. Even so, the very sight of it made

4

Mattie's stomach rumble. She'd missed lunch. And now it looked as though dinner wasn't going to be a part of the immediate future.

Detlinger smiled at her. "Help yourself to the fries. You're welcome to the burger too, but I think it's gone beyond the point where it's fit for anything but a decent burial."

"Thanks. I'm starving."

"Try the food first. You might want to skip the thanks."

With one hand on the wheel he gunned the engine and backed out of the drive. He grabbed the radio mike with his free hand, keyed it and informed the dispatcher that they were en route to Hennepin County Medical Center.

Detlinger spun the wheel hard and shot down Irving Avenue. "Find something to hold on to," he yelled. "I'll have you downtown in a couple of minutes." Moving into the traffic flow, he switched on the roof light bar and flasher. A few seconds later the siren kicked in, its urgent keening cutting open the solemn night quiet with a sharp-edged blade of sound, clearing a fast track through the sparse crosstown traffic. They sped past Lakewood Cemetery where the cruiser's flashing lights strobed the long shadows and made the tall, wrought-iron fence glow with an eerie incandescence.

Mattie tightened her grip on the padded door handle and swallowed a mouthful of fries. They were cold and stringy, with just a hint of potato taste buried under a heavy coating of salt. She grabbed another handful while Detlinger edged the patrol car up to sixty-five, then seventy.

Wiping her mouth, she glanced at Detlinger. He had both hands on the wheel now, his long, heavy fingers playing it lightly, almost caressing it. His eyes were narrow and bright; in the soft light of the dashboard his young-old face looked intent, like a true believer at a canvas-topped revival meeting.

"This man they took to the hospital. You said he'd been stabbed?"

Detlinger nodded, his eyes still locked on the road as they shot a red light on Nicollet. "I heard they found him over by

5

Lake Calhoun. Older guy . . . deaf. Pretty badly cut up. Somebody really did a job on him. They're still not sure if he's going to make it.''

"What kind of animal would do something like that?"

"I can think of a hundred or so offhand. But then I've only been on the force for a couple of years.''

"Is it really that bad?"

"Yes and no. It's a long way from being Detroit or Miami, but sometimes it seems like we're already there. I'd be happy with what we've got now. But it keeps getting worse. They're probably saving *better* for an election year.'' Detlinger frowned. "They sent me to pick you up because I happened to be a couple of blocks from your place when the call went out. The hospital phoned before dispatch contacted me, but your line was busy both times they tried, so I guess they figured you were home." He sounded a little puzzled over this last bit. The dark house, the attaché case, the grocery bag. It was obvious that Mattie herself had only just arrived.

She stared out at the darkness for a second, then smiled. "It must have been someone talking to my answering machine. Someone with a lot to say." She'd been meaning to disconnect the damn thing. She'd never liked the idea of a caller getting a disembodied, prerecorded voice when they'd dialed a *real* person. The machine had been a housewarming gift and now, after six weeks, it was about time for it to be broken beyond repair. Still, she wondered who'd called. Peter, long distance from New York? Or maybe his lawyer again? More likely than not, it had been her mother "just checking" to see how she was.

The speedometer needle hovered near seventy-five as they raced by the few remaining residential blocks and swung up the entrance ramp to Interstate 35-W where the siren and flashing lights quickly cleared the fast lane of all other traffic. Fighting a sudden wave of tiredness, Mattie closed her eyes for a moment and leaned her head back against the cold, plastic shield that sealed off the rear of the sedan. Muffled by the

6

siren's wail, the radio dispatcher's voice droned on incessantly with reports of the district's pursuits, requests and notices.

"This sign language stuff. You get paid for it?"

Mattie blinked and opened her eyes again. "The hospital pays for the interpreting. But I do some volunteer work too. Actually, I'm a teacher of the deaf. The interpreting is just a sideline."

"Is it hard to learn?"

"Not too hard, but it takes a lot of time and practice to do it well. If you're interested, District Two-eighty-seven, the place where I work, has a list of introductory courses. I think it would be great if there were some policemen around who could sign."

"I'll keep it in mind," Detlinger assured her. But something in his tone told Mattie that he probably wouldn't. She wasn't surprised. When she mentioned words like "time" and "practice," people's attention seemed to fall off and drift away.

They came out of a curve at high speed and Mattie saw the downtown skyline, a patchwork silhouette in granite and limestone, the older buildings, the ones she'd grown up with, dominated now by the IDS Center and the sterile blue glass facade of the Piper Jaffery Tower. In the foreground the graceful lines of a massive old church added a note of much-needed class, its impact only slightly diminished by the seedy red neon glow from the sign atop the nearby Hotel Lemmington. A little to the east, searchlights mounted at the peak of Foshay Tower cut through the murky night sky, the powerful yellow-white beams illuminating the ragged scud clouds that rode above the wind.

"Almost there."

Detlinger grinned as they shot off the highway at the Grant Street exit. Traffic was heavier downtown. The Vikings had a home game on and the Metrodome was just a block north of the Med Center. In spite of the congestion, Detlinger eased up only slightly on the gas. A few minutes and a couple of near misses later, he shut the siren down as they swung into the hospital's drive. Pulling to the curb just shy of the ambulance bays, Detlinger cut the engine and climbed out without a word. Mattie yanked the door open and ran after him.

2

The man on the narrow trauma bed was in a kind of limbo, hovering somewhere between old age and imminent death.

They'd cut away his blood-sodden shirt and folded it back to treat the wounds that crisscrossed his knobby chest like deep channels cut in some primitive relief map. Beneath a widow's peak of iron-gray hair, his face was long and thin, the skin stretched tight over ridges of bone, his coloring so pale he seemed almost translucent from loss of blood. The emergency room team had inserted chest and breathing tubes and had hooked him up to two large central IV lines and a cardiac monitor. A plastic ID band dangled from one bony wrist with his name spelled out on it in capital letters: KENDRICK, NOAH. In spite of all the medical apparatus, his chest rose and fell in a broken rhythm, as though breathing were more an act of memory than respiration. His body moved from time to time, but only his eyes seemed truly alive. Mattie couldn't explain it, but they had a *look* to them. As though they were being fueled by something burning and bright just behind the muddy brown irises.

"His blood pressure's dropping."

"Hang another unit of O-negative and repack the wounds. Where in the hell *is* that surgeon?"

"On his way."

"Doc, the interpreter's here." A police lieutenant whose name was Ryder grasped Mattie by the elbow and pushed her forward.

"All right," the ER resident muttered. "I can *see* her."

As if to prove the point, he turned and focused his bleary-eyed gaze on Mattie. He was a dark-haired, heavyset young man dressed in rumpled surgical greens spotted with dry blood. There was a certain tightness around his mouth and eyes, a haunted look that probably came from having had to pull up too many sheets over too many faces. He smiled at Mattie tentatively. But the smile faded when he looked down at Kendrick again.

"He's been trying to tell us something. Been at it ever since the paramedics brought him in. Moving his hands around so damned much he pulled the IV out twice. I almost had to put restraints on him. Go ahead. Find out what he has to say. Then maybe he'll be a little more cooperative."

Nodding, Mattie squeezed past the doctor and positioned herself at the side of the trauma bed. She leaned forward slightly so he could see the signs more clearly, then introduced herself as the interpreter, tension suddenly making her fingers stiff and awkward as she formed the familiar signs. But she could tell from the change in Kendrick's face that he understood what she was signing.

"Ask him who attacked him," Ryder said.

"Who attacked you?" she signed.

The brightness in the deaf man's eyes intensified as he tracked the movements of Mattie's hands. With a visible effort, he slowly raised his own. As he turned them toward her, Mattie saw that both palms were deeply lacerated and that the long, spatulate fingers were caked with dry blood. Kendrick leveled his right hand in Mattie's direction, index and forefinger extended like the barrel of a make-believe gun. He was fingerspelling the letter *h*.

Mattie watched, stringing the letters together as they formed words and the words a sentence. "House . . . burned . . . down," she voiced it softly. "No . . . iron . . . man . . . there." Kendrick's thin lips pulled back in a pain-etched parody of a smile. He let his hands fall back to the bed covers.

"Is that it?" Ryder demanded.

10

"That's all he said."

"It doesn't make any sense. Ask him again. Ask who attacked him."

Mattie signed the question again. She was sure that Kendrick was reading her clearly, sure that he understood.

Kendrick stubbornly shook his head. He raised his hands again. They were trembling now, the blood-daubed fingers fluttering like branches in the wind. He clenched his teeth, willing his hands to steady themselves. When he finally had them under control, he tipped the right one toward Mattie, index and forefinger extended, just like before.

"House," Mattie voiced the words again. "Burned . . . "

"The surgeon's here. He's scrubbing now."

"Just a few more seconds," Ryder protested. "If I could just . . . "

The young resident shoved him aside. "All right," he yelled, "let's get him up to OR *stat*."

The lighting in the Med Center's cafeteria was subdued, almost dim. Mattie found it soothing, like a stiff drink after a long, hard day or a Valium at bedtime. The place was nicely laid out, with a lot of space between the individual tables, as though the hospital wanted to save its patrons the embarrassment of contamination. There was room enough to avoid brushing up against someone else's grief, to keep you from making too close an acquaintance with a stranger's death. It was nice though, pleasant. But still not a room where you'd want to spend a lot of time.

Sitting at a small table along the wall, Mattie sipped coffee and stared down at the remains of her meal. The French onion soup had begun to congeal, an oily coating spreading over its murky brown depths. Her salad still looked fresh, but the the massive slab of apple pie she'd selected for dessert had begun to ooze, the slowly sinking crust now holding all the appeal of damp cardboard. The food was fine when she'd bought it. But after two bites of salad she'd shoved the tray away, her

11

stomach bilious and heaving. The tray was still there. No one had come by to collect it yet. But she'd lost her appetite somewhere between the emergency room and the cafeteria.

"Thanks for waiting, Miss Shayne."

Mattie looked up to see Lieutenant Ryder standing in front of her, holding a coffee cup and saucer in each of his blunt-fingered hands. She smiled. "No problem, Lieutenant. I figured Mr. Kendrick might need me again."

"You look like you could use a refill." He set one of the coffees down in front of her, put her empty cup on the tray, then shoved the whole thing on a nearby table before settling into the chair across from Mattie's.

He looked at her for a second then glanced down at the steaming dark liquid in the cup. "Kendrick died on the table," he said quietly. "There wasn't a hell of a lot they could do for him. Shock-trauma combined with all that loss of blood. The doctor said he was surprised he hung on as long as he did." Ryder sighed, tore open a couple of Sweet 'n Lows and dumped the contents in his coffee. He stirred it noisily and slammed the spoon down on the table.

Mattie didn't know what to say. She'd only known the old man for a few minutes, maybe the last important minutes of his life. She was surprised at the sense of loss she felt. Almost as though it were the death of a longtime friend. Her stomach suddenly felt tight. She could feel something cold kiss the back of her neck like a breath of winter wind.

"Was he married? Did he have a family?"

Ryder studied her for a long, quiet moment, as if he were weighing out beforehand exactly how much he was and wasn't going to tell her.

"He was married," he said finally. "He had a wedding ring on when they brought him in. Also his wife's name and their home number were on one of those 'in case of emergency' cards in his wallet. I don't know if they had any kids. What he *did* have was three major credit cards and eighty-seven dollars in cash. So that pretty much eliminates this as being

12

a robbery-mugging that got out of hand.'' Ryder shook his head. ''You know it's odd, but in twenty-two years on the force I don't think I've ever been involved in a homicide investigation where the victim was deaf.''

Mattie took a tentative sip of her coffee. ''Do you think his deafness might have something to do with his murder?''

Ryder shrugged. ''Maybe yes. Maybe no. It's early days yet. There's a lot of ground to cover before we start theorizing. My partner's out at the scene now. After I find out what he's got, I have to locate Kendrick's wife. We've been trying to get a hold of her, but no luck so far. I have to break the news to her. It's not my favorite part of the job.''

''It must be hard.''

''There are a number of things I don't like about being a cop. That's the only one I really hate.''

Mattie nodded but didn't say anything. There wasn't anything she could say.

Ryder looked nearly as tired as she felt. There was a certain hollowness around his blue-gray eyes that attested to too many nights of missed sleep, not just recently but over a great many years. He was pushing fifty, Mattie calculated, maybe even past it. Tall and broad-shouldered, he was heavy without being fat. Even the subdued lighting of the cafeteria couldn't mask the silver threading in his wavy brown hair. Beneath it his face was thickset and angular, the lines of it softened slightly by a mottled gray-brown beard. The one thing that surprised Mattie was how well he was dressed. Immaculately conservative in a custom-tailored gray tweed three-piece suit with a crisp white oxford cloth shirt and a silk foulard tie. She'd always had a different image of a police detective. Something more along the lines of Columbo, who looked like an abused archery target in his disreputable trench coat. Ryder reminded her more of a college professor or maybe a minor diplomat, somehow gone astray.

He smiled at her and formed a steeple with his thick-fingered hands. ''House burned down,'' he said thoughtfully. ''No iron man there. That's a damn strange dying message. It doesn't make any sense. I've already made a few phone calls and the only major fire reported tonight is a barn that burned down over at the stockyards in St. Paul. And I don't have *any* idea what he meant about the 'iron man' not being there. Now it's nothing personal,'' he said locking eyes with Mattie, ''but are you positive you understand exactly what he was saying?''

''Absolutely. He finger-spelled each letter of each word. It's slow but accurate. In sign language, it's kind of the equivalent of writing it out in big block letters.''

''That's an interesting coincidence. According to his business cards, he had his own printing company, Kendrick and Cole Graphics.''

''It's not unusual, though. There are a lot of deaf people in the printing trade. They teach it at most of the residential schools. In fact, some of the best printers in the country are deaf.''

Ryder took a sip of his coffee then smiled at her. ''You seem to know a lot about this stuff.''

Mattie laughed. ''Sometimes it *sounds* like I do. I guess I know quite a bit, but not as much as I'd like to. It's a big field. There's always something to learn.''

''It's the same with police work. They're always improving things, finding new and better ways to do it. Just when I finally get comfortable with the old way, some bastard comes along and *improves* it. Irritates the hell out of me. Most things don't need improving, they need to be left alone.''

''Maybe. Do you always swear that much?''

He grinned at her over the rim of his cup. ''Always. It's an integral part of my hard-boiled cop image. But I can drop it if it bothers you.''

''I think I can live with it,'' she said smiling. It really didn't bother her. In fact, it reminded her of one of her all-time favorite people, her Uncle Red, a retired bootlegger who'd recently married a nineteen-year-old Sioux girl from the reservation down by Shakopee.

14

In the brief silence that followed, Mattie looked around the room. Across the way a woman in a cheap cloth coat was crying, her face pressed against a wrinkled bandanna, thin shoulders rising and falling in a jerky, broken rhythm. Sitting next to her, a gray-haired man with a raw-boned, weathered farmer's face was staring straight ahead, pale eyes looking inward, or maybe out, not seeing anything at all. The collar of his red and black mackinaw was turned up; smoke from a neglected cigarette drifted up and around his face like incense from some dark and private altar.

Mattie was conscious of staring too long. Feeling like an intruder, she swallowed hard and quickly looked away.

"Now about this sign language stuff," Ryder continued. "We tried to get him to write it out when they first brought him in but his hands were too badly lacerated to hold a pencil. You say he 'finger-spelled' the words. Is there some other way he could have done it?"

Mattie nodded. "There are two basic forms of sign language, Signed English and American Sign Language. The first is like spoken English with all the right word endings and everything in its proper grammatical order. ASL is something else again. It's structured differently from English, usually with the most important word at the beginning of the sentence. Finish eat noon," she said as an example, signing along as she spoke. "It's a very direct form of communication. It also relies a great deal on facial expression and the emphasis with which a sign is made. And it has its own slang, which varies from one part of the country to another."

Leaning back, Ryder took out a crumpled pack of Pall Malls and lit one. They were sitting in the nonsmoking section. Either he hadn't noticed or he was just too tired to care.

"Where does the finger-spelling fit in?"

"It's used in both systems, mostly for spelling out proper names, things there aren't any signs for. It's a manual alphabet with hand positions for each of the twenty-six letters."

Ryder frowned. "Why do you think he chose that particular method? The others sound easier."

15

"Accuracy," Mattie said after a moment's hesitation. "Spelling it out letter by letter by letter, he was able to convey *exactly* what he wanted to say. That's very important in sign language because so many signs have more than one meaning. Like fire and burn. There's only one sign for both."

"That's interesting, but it still doesn't make Kendrick's dying words any easier to understand. Why couldn't he have said something simple like . . . 'my brother-in-law knifed me'? A clear, dying declaration that I could get an arrest warrant with."

"Maybe he didn't know who stabbed him?"

Ryder grunted. "Believe it or not, Miss Shayne, the thought had crossed my mind."

"I'm not trying to tell you your job," Mattie said defensively. She was too tired to put up with any of this condescension crap, particularly when she had an important point to make. "Think about Kendrick's last words for a minute," she continued. "He made two statements, one about a house that burned down and one about an iron man that wasn't there. They don't tell us *who* killed him but rather *why* he was killed. Maybe he figured that once you knew the reason or reasons why he was murdered you'd also know who'd done it."

"Praise the Lord. Ellery Queen's on the case."

"It's possible," Mattie insisted. In the nearly empty cafeteria her voice sounded far too loud. Across the room a couple of nurses turned, their crisp, starched whites rustling as they eyed Mattie with a sudden clinical interest.

"All right," Ryder sighed. "It's possible."

"Especially in the context of deafness and sign language. Deaf people have a tendency to be very direct. Kendrick was dying so he said the two most important things about his death. Unembellished but very vital facts."

"But they still don't make any sense. Unless you know something I don't?"

"Sorry." Mattie shook her head.

Ryder took a final drag off his cigarette and let the butt

16

sputter out in his saucer where spilled coffee surrounded the cup like a tiny gray-brown moat. "With any luck," he said, "we'll get something from the the scene. Physical evidence or maybe even an eyewitness. Somebody jogging around the lake who saw the killer. With all that bloodshed he couldn't have walked away clean." Ryder drained his coffee cup and pushed back his chair. "Thanks for your time, Miss Shayne. I really do appreciate it. I'll need a statement from you. I can send someone over to your place to take it tomorrow if that's convenient?"

"Fine. It's Saturday and I'll be home all day. Sleeping."

"Can I drop you somewhere now?"

"Home. Thirty-third and Irving. If it's not out of your way."

"I go right by there."

"About Kendrick's widow?" Mattie said hesitantly. "Is she hearing or do you have another interpreter lined up for the job?"

"You're saying she might be deaf?"

"It's a strong possibility."

"Meaning I might need an interpreter?"

"Unless you were thinking of using flash cards." It came out angrier than she'd intended, but there was no taking it back now. "Listen, Lieutenant, I'm just trying to help, not tell you how to do your job. There's a good chance that Mrs. Kendrick is either deaf or hearing impaired. Deaf people often marry other deaf people for all the obvious reasons. Now she might be hearing or a lip reader with good speech. But you can't count on that. When you tried to contact her by phone, were there any letters in front of the number?"

Ryder nodded. "I can't remember what they were, though. The hospital handled all the phoning; they're supposed to page me as soon as they get someone on the line."

"Those letters in front of the number are probably TDD. It's an abbreviation for a printer that uses the phone lines to transmit and receive messages and conversation. They're in fairly common use among the deaf and hearing impaired. Of course, you need a TDD in order to contact another TDD user. I know the hospital has several for emergency situations like this."

Ryder stared down at his shoes, shifting uncomfortably. Apologies obviously weren't easy for him. "Then she probably *is* deaf?"

"Not necessarily. They'd have the TDD for him, in any case. But then again, she may well be."

"I'm sorry," Ryder said quietly. "If you can tolerate my company for another hour or two, I'd really appreciate you coming along. I've got to stop at the crime scene first, though. But I could drop you at your place, then pick you up when I'm done."

Mattie shook her head. "If you need an interpreter, you've got one, but I'd better stick with you until we're done. Because if I get within three feet of my couch, that's gonna be it for the night."

"Thanks," Ryder said grinning. "Let's get going then."

The cafeteria was closing as they left. The lights blinked out over the long steam table and service counter. A janitor began to stack the chairs while another one slapped at the floor with a dripping mop. Ryder's gleaming oxfords made a loud hollow sound on the tiles.

There's a lot of anger there, Mattie thought. He even *walks* angry.

As they stood waiting for the elevator, she stared at her blurred reflection in the brushed chrome doors. Her dark blond hair was windblown and wild; her face was tight and drawn, pale under the soft, warm light. She looked like an aging starlet on the skids, someone at an open casting call for *Night of the living Dead*. She had to start getting more sleep. Otherwise, people were going to begin mistaking her for her mother.

Ryder cleared his throat, took out his cigarettes and then shoved them back in his pocket. "If I was a little abrupt back there, please don't take it personally," he said. "It's been a tough year for everyone in the Division. Right now it looks

18

as though we're gonna have a record-breaking number of homicides, big figures in the other major crime areas too. I'm working so many case files that sometimes I wonder if I'll ever see the top of my desk again." Looking down at Mattie, he smiled and shook his head. "Why am I telling you my troubles? You probably got enough of your own."

"I don't mind," Mattie insisted. "It gives me a good excuse to dump all my problems on you later. Not that I ever needed a good excuse." She grinned at Ryder and then looked away, glancing at her distorted reflection in the metal doors. "You take it very personally, don't you?"

"If you mean my job," Ryder replied, "I take it *very* seriously, *very* personally. I wouldn't want to be in Homicide-Robbery if I didn't. It's a real pressure cooker. I've seen it burn out a lot of good cops. But it's also where the action is. There isn't anything I know of that can be tougher, more challenging than a murder investigation."

"I have a feeling you must be good at it."

Shrugging, Ryder looked away. "There are better," he muttered, "but I don't do too bad."

"You have any deaf friends? Know any deaf people at all?"

"No, not really. All I know about deafness is what you told me tonight. But I'm interested in any background information you can give me."

Mattie bit her lower lip and stared thoughtfully at a nonexistent point just beyond Ryder's shoulder. "Now, I don't *know* the Kendricks," she said finally. "And I'm still not sure I shouldn't save this for later. But there are some deaf people who consider themselves a part of a separate culture, a culture that doesn't have much in common with the hearing world. Their lives tend to center around *being* deaf. Their spouses, closest friends, the people who know them best would most likely be deaf too. I wouldn't call these deaf people *anti*-hearing; you can't make generalities about any group of individuals. But there is a certain amount of anger there, a very strong sense of separation. If Noah Kendrick was like that, you could wind up learning a lot about deafness on this case."

"You make them sound almost militant."

"Some of them are. Particularly in Kendrick's age group. Whatever schooling he had would have been back in the era when sign language wasn't as widely accepted as it is today. There were certain oral schools, not the good ones, but some, where students who tried to sign had their knuckles slapped with a ruler or their hands tied behind their backs. Some educators wanted the deaf to pass themselves off as hearing rather than try 'total communication,'—sign, lip reading, speech, whatever works for the individual student."

"I never knew that went on," Ryder said slowly. "I can see where they'd be bitter, justifiably so." Shaking his head, he prodded the elevator button with a stiff forefinger. "Next," he said, "you'll be telling me the killer might be deaf."

Mattie shrugged. "Why not? Didn't I read somewhere that in a large percentage of homicides the killer and the victim are known to each other? If the dead man were black, I don't think you'd be so quick to dismiss another black as a possible murderer."

"All right." Ryder held up his hands signaling surrender. "Maybe it is a possibility, but in all my years on the force I've never arrested a deaf person for *anything*, let alone murder. I'm not denying you have a point, but it still doesn't sit right with me."

"That's because you're thinking more about the disability than the people who have it. The deaf are, to quote a much-hackneyed phrase, 'just like everyone else.' Good, bad and all the stops in between with their share of both victims *and* villains." Mattie slid her right index finger under her left palm and then out toward the left with a twist, the same kind you give a knife when it's deeply imbedded.

"What the hell was that?"

Mattie smiled. "It's one of the easier signs to learn. It's the sign for murder."

3

"No comment."

"Why?"

"Because there's nothing to comment *on* yet."

"Have you identified the . . . "

"You know the procedure," Ryder said wearily. "The victim's name will be released after we've notified the next of kin. Phone the precinct later tonight. We should have something for you then."

Politely but firmly, Ryder shouldered his way past the pretty, blond newscaster, turning his back on the bright lights and whirring minicams. He held Mattie's arm as they picked their way through a maze of ground cables and through the small crowd that ringed the mobile news van. The newscaster's clear, well-modulated voice followed them, carried along on the wind.

"Early this evening on the shore of Lake Calhoun, an unidentified man was fatally . . . "

Self-consciously Mattie poked at her wind-tangled hair. "I hope I'm not going to be on the ten o'clock news."

"Don't worry about it," Ryder grinned. "I didn't give them anything they could use."

"You have something against the media?"

"No. Not as long as they let me do my job." Without breaking stride he dug out a laminated ID card and clipped it to the breast pocket of his jacket. "Most of them are pretty good about it. They know how important the first few hours of an investigation are; that they're the best shot we've got at pulling all the elements together while everything is still fresh.

21

After we've done all the groundwork, I'm always willing to tell the press what I can. Why not?'' he said, shrugging. "They've helped us crack a lot of cases by broadcasting descriptions of the suspects." He glanced back at the mobile news van. They were packing up, anxious now to get back to the studio. "There are times," Ryder sighed. "But as much as I'd like to, you can't ignore an outlet like that."

As they neared the lake the wind grew stronger, a steady blast edged with a biting cold and unbroken except by a few bare, gray-brown trees. Patrol cars and unmarked police sedans blocked off the intersection of Thirty-second Street and the East Calhoun Parkway, their flashing red lights spilling random color over shadow-dappled lawns and houses. They passed a knot of shivering but determined gawkers, crossed the two-lane parkway and mounted the curb on the opposite side. A patrolman was stationed there, at the top of the stairs that formed the Thirty-second Street entrance to the lakefront park. He nodded to Ryder, grinned and rubbed his gloved hands together. Under the visored uniform cap his square face was red from the cold. Droplets of glittering frost hung from the corners of his bushy, black mustache.

"It's a hell of a night for it, Lieutenant."

"That's for damn sure. I don't even want to *think* about what kind of winter we're in for." Ryder shook his head, tugged his jacket collar up and jammed his hands into his pockets. "Who's doing the house to house, Tom?"

"Macklin and Bonnetie. So far they haven't . . . "

Mattie tuned out the rest of the conversation. Stepping up to the knee-high guardrail, she peered down at the scene below. Pole-mounted portable lights illuminated the steep, overgrown slope that led down to the bicycle and pedestrian paths, a narrow strip of beach and the dark, wind-creased expanse of Lake Calhoun itself. The garish white light made everything stand out in sharp relief. Trees, clumps of saw grass and weeds, two Port-O-Johns and the rickety lifeguard stand all looked as though they'd been cut away from the darkness with a fine-edged engraver's tool. A half-dozen plainclothes detectives and forensic technicians labored under the lights. Mattie watched two of them as they climbed up-slope, carefully combing the tangled underbrush for clues. Another, making notations on a clipboard, looked up suddenly and smiled at Mattie. After a second's hesitation she smiled back. The scene below reminded her of an archaeological dig she'd once visited. It was a good analogy, she decided. Only these men were searching for traces of recent death instead of the buried remains of some long-ago civilization.

Ryder tugged at her sleeve. "I've got to go down and talk to my partner. You want to come along or wait up here?"

The patrolman at the top of the stairs lifted a plastic ribbon of tape. It was one of four lengths that marked off the wide, square perimeters of the crime scene. The warning POLICE LINE DO NOT CROSS was printed all along it, as though constant repetition might somehow compensate for the barrier's patent flimsiness. Ducking beneath it, Mattie followed Ryder down the patched concrete steps. The wind off the lake was brutal. Fearful of loosing her footing, Mattie held tight to the weathered wooden railing while using her free hand to anchor down her billowing coattails and skirt. As they neared the bottom of the stairs, a thin, white-haired man in wrinkled chinos and a poplin windbreaker ambled over to meet them.

"I was wondering when you were going to show up. You bring any coffee?" He smiled at Mattie. "He never brings coffee."

Ryder sighed. "Kiefer, this is Mattie Shayne. Miss Shayne, my partner, Al Kiefer."

"Nice to meet you, Mattie." His smile creased up at the corners, forming a wolfish grin. He looked pale, almost spectral under the glaring lights. He reminded Mattie of some minor character out of Dickens. With his spiky white hair, papery skin and hawkish features he resembled a ghost. Maybe the one they left out of *A Christmas Carol*. The ghost of Christmases best forgotten.

"Miss Shayne interpreted for us at the Med Center," Ryder explained. "She's coming with me out to Kendrick's house, just in case the wife is deaf too."

"Makes sense," Kiefer said. "What did you get at the hospital?"

"Just a couple of phrases, neither of them what I'd call illuminating." He repeated Noah Kendrick's dying message.

"I hate it when they go all cryptic like that," Kiefer grumbled. Shaking his head, he took out a pack of Larks and hunching his thin shoulders against the wind, finally managed to connect one with the sputtering flame of his lighter. He took a deep drag on it and exhaled smoke through hooked nostrils. "None of that ties in with what I've got so far."

"Which is?"

"The murder weapon for one," he said cheerfully. "You want to take a look at it? I don't think Detlinger's sent it downtown yet." Without waiting for a reply, he turned and loped down the bicycle path, heading toward where a heavyset man was hunched over a big aluminum carrying case. In motion, Kiefer looked like a gangly teenager who hadn't quite yet picked up the knack of running. His sneakered feet slapped the tarmac in an uneven rhythm, crunching a path through the brittle, windblown leaves.

"Interesting man," Mattie commented.

Ryder smiled, rubbing some circulation back into his stiff, red hands. "I don't think anyone's ever called him that before. Most people go right for *weird*. But, like him or not, he's a hell of a good detective."

"I like him," Mattie said defensively.

"Terrific."

Ignoring him, Mattie turned and looked out over the lake. With three and a half miles of shoreline, Calhoun was the largest of the thirty-some lakes within the borders of Minneapolis-St. Paul. She'd spent a dozen summers growing up here, swimming and sailing, trying unsuccessfully for the perfect tan and even more unsuccessfully for the attention of a certain

24

curly-haired lifeguard. But tonight the lake was different. A grim backdrop to death, a cold and foreign place that had nothing to do with childhood memories. She bunched the cloth in her coat pockets around her freezing hands and watched the dark, wind-roiled water as it surged up over the narrow strip of dirty sand. Off to her right, small boats and catamarans rode out the angry chop, hulls banging against the docksides, masts and lines straining against the force of the wind. A little farther down she could make out the shadowed bulk of the peaked-roof refreshment pavilion, its windows shuttered and dark. Mattie shifted her gaze, looking across the lake to where the lights from the old Calhoun Beach Club smeared the water's edge with shimmering brush strokes of vibrant yellow and white. The distant lights conjured up an illusion of brightness and warmth. But their radiant glow only made the rest of the lake appear colder and more desolate than before.

"I've got it," Kiefer said as he came panting back down the bicycle path. "Take a look at this." Grinning, he held out an eighteen by twelve corrugated cardboard mount. Beneath a protective plastic covering, the loops of twine secured a wooden-handled kitchen knife to the flat surface while minimizing any possible damage to prints. The tapering knife blade was about seven inches long. A few scattered patches of bare metal caught and reflected the light. The rest of it was mottled with dark, dry blood.

Mattie shivered, looked out at the lake again and then, reluctantly, back at the knife. It was ugly, macabre, but she couldn't keep her eyes off it.

"All right," Ryder nodded thoughtfully. "Where did you find it?"

"Up in the bushes near the top." Kiefer turned and gestured up-slope toward the low, wooden railing at street level. "I've seen this type of knife around," he continued. "It's imported, expensive as these things go. Made by Sabatier in France. The blade is high carbon stainless steel. Real first-class cutlery."

"So what do we do now? Put out an all points for the Galloping Gourmet?"

" 'Fraid not.'' Frowning, Kiefer tapped the cardboard mount with a bony fingertip. "You can buy these all over the country. A lot of department stores and specialty cookware places carry the line. I expect you could pick up this little item in a dozen or more stores around the Cities."

Studying the blood-encrusted blade, Ryder lit a cigarette and then shoved his hands back into his pockets in a futile effort to keep warm. The relentless wind had tousled his gray-brown hair, but with the exception of his turned up collar, he remained impeccably turned out. "Well now," he said finally. "We have what appears to be the murder weapon. There probably aren't any prints on it. There never are. But at least it's something."

"What it is," Kiefer quietly corrected him, "is the good news. The *bad* news is that this isn't the crime scene. Just a convenient dumping ground for a dying man."

"Shit." A load of frustration and anger came out along with the word. A half-second later Ryder's face began to redden. He glanced apologetically at Mattie. "Sorry," he muttered.

"I'm a schoolteacher," she said smiling. "I hear a lot worse than that, usually *before* my morning coffee break. There's even a sign for that particular word." She wrapped one shivering hand around the thumb of the other and then yanked the thumb out. The sign was as graphic as it was obvious.

Kiefer's shrill laughter was carried off on the wind. "I'll have to remember that," he said. "It's perfect for the next time I have to go see the chief." His face became serious again as his dark eyes shifted back to Ryder. "Let me run this scenario by you and you see if there's anything that doesn't fit. Around twilight, Kendrick, already critically wounded, was pitched over the railing just to the right of the stairs. The momentum of the fall carries him downhill through the weeds and grass. We found traces of blood all the way down from the point of impact but not enough in one place for this to be the scene. Now when Kendrick hits bottom he still has enough strength left to crawl out of the underbrush. He scares the

26

living hell out of some lady zooming by on a ten-speed. She phones for an ambulance. She says she didn't see anyone else, just the victim. Whoever dumped Kendrick was probably long gone by then.''

In unison both men turned and looked up at the street above them where Thirty-second Street dead-ended into East Calhoun Parkway. At that same point the parkway narrowed to two single lanes separated by a grass and concrete median for the pedestrian traffic using the stairs down to the beach. Wood and stucco houses lined the far side of the road, most of them prewar single family units with second-story porches and sun decks built to take advantage of the lakefront view. But trees on both sides of the parkway obstructed a clear line of vision from numerous angles. It was surprising how many points there were from which you *couldn't* see the stairs or the overgrown slope alongside them. And of course there had to be someone around to do the seeing. Thousands of people came here during the warm summer months. But on a blustery weekday in late October, that number was reduced to a handful of die-hard joggers and cyclists.

"Risky," Ryder said finally.

"But a well-calculated risk. Especially if you happen to be driving a panel truck or a van, one of the newer ones with the sliding door on the passenger side." Kiefer peered up at the dark street above them, his dark eyes narrow and intense like a psychic trying to pick up the ghostly afterglow of the dear departed. "The pedestrian crossway is right there at the head of the stairs," he continued. "And the locals are used to seeing vehicles stop there all the time. It would only take a matter of seconds to open the passenger door, shove Kendrick out and over the rail and then toss the murder weapon out after him. Now the ambulance dispatcher logged the call in at six twenty-two. It was already getting dark then. There wasn't all that much chance of the killer being seen unless there was another vehicle directly behind his. And as long as everything took place on the passenger side, the car or van itself obstructed the view from the houses across the way. Glancing up-slope again, Kiefer frowned and shook his head. "From down here the angles are all wrong. You might get a glimpse of someone standing right at the railing, but a few feet back, no way."

"So our killer doesn't mind taking chances." Ryder didn't sound at all pleased with the realization.

"Let's not underestimate his intelligence, though," Kiefer said smiling grimly. "Kendrick was already dying, a deaf man whose hands were too badly cut up to hold a pencil, a man who could only communicate with someone who understood sign language. Our perpetrator calculated the odds and decided to dump Kendrick before he was dead. He took a small risk in doing it *here* but then I don't see him driving all over Minneapolis looking for just the right spot." Kiefer sighed. "I don't like this case. I'm cold. I'm tired. And as soon as I'm finished here I'm going home to bed."

"Drink something hot and take a couple of aspirins," Mattie suggested. Kiefer looked sick. Under the ruddy flush of the wind, his pale face had taken on a decidedly grayish tinge. His eyes were moist and shining, usually a sure sign of the flu.

"I think that's just what I'll do," he said grinning weakly at Mattie.

"Take care of yourself," Ryder advised him. "I'll call you in the morning." He peered at his watch. Under the glaring lights, the reflection off the crystal made him squint; he angled his wrist around trying in vain to read the hands and numbers. "The hell with it," he muttered, letting his arm drop back to his side. "It's *always* later than you think. We'd better get out to Kendrick's place and break the news to the widow." An edge of bitterness had crept into his voice. It surprised Mattie. And for some odd reason disappointed her too.

"Nice to meet you, Miss Shayne." Kiefer managed a feeble smile.

"Likewise. Don't forget about those aspirin."

"Have you two been partners long?" she asked Ryder as they walked up the stairs from the beach.

28

"A little over a year. We get on all right," he added after a moment's hesitation. "It's sort of like a marriage. It takes a certain amount of time to settle into it. I was eight years with Tim Reardon, my partner before Kiefer."

"What happened to him?"

"He shot himself in the head," Ryder said quietly.

Mattie didn't know what to say to that. She finally decided that nothing was better than some stupid platitude. At the top of the stairs, she glanced back for one last look at the dark, angry water. Why would anyone want to murder Noah Kendrick? What possible threat could a frail and aging deaf man be? And what had he been trying to tell them before he died? A house that had burned down? An iron man who wasn't there? She had to admit that Ryder was right. None of it made the slightest bit of sense.

Mattie shivered. She was too tired to think. Willing her mind to take a rest, she tuned out everything except the wail of the wind through the treetops. She probably just imagined it, but the wind seemed to grow louder, more blatantly destructive during their long, silent walk back to the car.

4

At first Mattie thought that they'd misread the address. The house didn't quite fit in with the image she'd been forming of Noah Kendrick. Not that she'd expected something *seedy*, just someplace less respectable, less grand. As Ryder leaned forward to stub out a cigarette in the overflowing ashtray, Mattie glanced at the notebook lying open on the seat. Looking up again she checked the number against the one by the door. So much for preconceived notions. Whether she wanted to believe it or not, this was where Kendrick had lived.

The house was a gabled, twenties Tudor with freshly painted cream-colored stucco and dark, decorative half-timbering. Like its neighbors on either side, it was set back from the street on the crest of a sloping hillside. The wide lawn in front was trim and immaculate, a *very* distant relative to Mattie's own leaf-littered patch of scrub grass. Two stately paper birch trees dominated the yard, their slender branches snapping and groaning as they cast flickering ribbons of shadow over the house and drive. Behind the wind-bent branches, the second-story windows of the house were all dark but on the floor below, a soft glow was visible through the sheer white curtains. More light, warm and yellow, spilled from the polished brass coach lamps flanking the front door. Mattie's eyes were drawn to them, but after a moment she forced herself to look away. The porch lights were burning for Noah Kendrick. His wife didn't know it yet, but he wasn't going to be coming home.

Ryder swung the unmarked sedan into the driveway, parked it and pocketed the keys. He made no move to get out of the car. Instead, he just sat there, staring at the house through the dirty windshield while Mattie leaned back and closed her eyes. She almost drifted off, but tired as she was, she wasn't about to fall asleep in a police car. When she sat up and reached for the door handle, Ryder put a restraining hand on her shoulder, his fingers light, barely touching the fabric of her coat. "About this interpreting thing," he said frowning.

"What about it, Lieutenant?"

He shifted uncomfortably, not quite able to meet her eyes. "I'm still a bit confused," he admitted finally. "We never did have a chance to go over this at the hospital. But if she is deaf . . . if we do have to use you, I'd better know a little more about how interpreting works. Because I'm going to have to ask Kendrick's wife a lot of questions and until she's proven otherwise, she's a suspect herself. So it's really important that the lines of communication don't," he hesitated, "don't get tangled up."

In the darkness Mattie gave him what she hoped was a reassuring smile. "There shouldn't be any problem. Working with an interpreter is really very simple. Just talk as you normally would. I'll translate everything into sign language. Everything *she* signs, I'll translate verbally for you. You might find it disconcerting at first, because even though you're doing all the talking her attention will be focused on me. But you'll get used to it. There's a lot more I could tell you, but that pretty well covers the basics."

"It sounds easy enough," Ryder said. But he didn't sound entirely convinced. Turning away, he shoved open the car door and eased his bulk up from the narrow seat. "Maybe I'll get lucky," he muttered under his breath. "Maybe she won't be deaf."

The sting of the wind on her face revived Mattie. The night air smelled sweet and fresh after the close, smoky confinement of Ryder's sedan. As she hurried to catch up with him, Ryder stopped abruptly beside the only other car in the driveway, a three-year-old Chrysler Le Baron. Its exterior reflected the same meticulous care as the house and grounds; in spite of the brutal Minnesota winters, the dark maroon paint and polished chrome were still gleaming, nearly factory fresh. Although she wasn't about to check it out, Mattie had a feeling that the engine under the hood was equally well cared for. She watched as Ryder leaned over and peered into the shadowed interior. Then, shaking his head, he straightened up and continued on by, trailing a broad hand over the shining hood in passing.

At the front door, Ryder paused for a second, listening, getting the feel of the place. Then he pushed the bell. There was no ringing sound, but through the sheer curtains they saw a bright flash of light.

It took Ryder by surprise, but Mattie had been expecting it. The device was common in deaf households, the flashing light a visual cue that took the place of the standard bell or buzzer. In the world of the deaf there were no such things as doorbells. They waited another thirty seconds before they heard the footsteps, a muffled tread barely audible above the whisper of the wind. The woman's face appeared suddenly, startling Mattie. She stepped back a pace, unnerved by the sheer intensity of the dark, narrowed eyes staring at them from behind the tiny window in the door.

"Police," Ryder said in a loud, carrying voice. Flipping open a pocket-size leather folder, he held it up so she could clearly see his gold detective's shield. Simultaneously Mattie formed the letter *c* with her fingers, positioning it over her heart. It was one of the easiest signs to remember. The *c* was for cop and its placement signified where uniformed officers wore their badges.

The face disappeared, absorbed by the darkness within. After a few seconds of silence Mattie heard the sharp, metallic snap of a bolt being drawn back. There was a tentative tugging from inside; then the heavy door swung open.

If the house hadn't been what Mattie expected, the woman was even more of a surprise.

She was twenty-three, maybe twenty-four. Certainly no older than that. Tall, almost boyishly slender, her long legs

33

were sheathed in tight, paint-smeared Levi's topped with an oversized man's shirt of soft, powder blue flannel with patch pockets that emphasized the contours of her small, upturned breasts. Her hair was cut fashionably short, thick and glossy, its color matched the deep ebon black of her eyes. Her face was sharp and hawkish with slanting, broad-bladed cheek-bones, a narrow nose and a generous mouth. She should have been ugly but she wasn't. Somehow the discordent features and the coltish body combined to give her a sensuous, predatory kind of beauty. She looked more like Kendrick's daughter than his wife.

Smoothing down her wind-ruffled hair, she stared expectantly at Mattie. In the bright light her eyes were wary and gleaming.

"Mrs. Kendrick?" Mattie's signing echoed Ryder's question. The woman ignored him, all of her attention focusing in on Mattie's moving hands.

"Yes," she signed back. "I'm Mrs. Kendrick . . . Ariana Kendrick." As if to dispel any possible doubt, she tapped her thick gold wedding ring. It was the only jewelry she had on.

"I'm Lieutenant Ryder and this is Miss Shayne. She isn't a police officer. She's here as our interpreter, if we need her."

"We do," Mrs. Kendrick signed. "Unless you happen to be proficient in sign language yourself?"

Mattie interpreted the question and Ryder shook his head. "May we come in, please?" Catching the flow of it now, he waited while Mattie finished translating the request into sign.

"Is it about my husband? Has something happened to Noah?" Her long, tapered fingers cut the air with an almost physical force. Her face was still blank, cautiously neutral, but Mattie could see the tension in her shoulders and the corded muscles of her bare, smooth neck.

As Mattie voiced the question, Ryder nodded. "Yes, it's about Mr. Kendrick. May we come in?"

She hesitated for a moment, then stepped back and motioned them inside.

The dimly lit hallway was heavy with trapped heat. Mattie quickly unbuttoned her trench coat, fighting down a feeling of slow suffocation. The warm, stale air held the lingering scent of furniture polish intermingled with the sickly-sweet fragrance of chrysanthemums. As Mattie's eyes adjusted to the light, she noticed a vase of them on a small table just beyond the door. At Mrs. Kendrick's insistence, she slipped off her trench coat and let the deaf woman hang it on an ornate Victorian rack. The walls were papered, but in the murky half-light, Mattie only got a vague impression of a fading floral pattern.

There was a stairway off to her right and midway down the opposite wall, an arched opening that led into the living room. Her gaze drifted past it and then back again. The man hadn't been there a second ago. But now he was, his stocky figure clearly outlined by a pale wash of light.

As they moved down the corridor, he stepped forward, spreading his heavy arms in a questioning gesture. Mrs. Kendrick shook her head and made the sign for police.

"What's this all about?" the man demanded. He was looking directly at Ryder now. In the narrow confines of the hall, his voice was loud and strident. Even from a distance Mattie could smell the bourbon on his breath.

"Police business," Ryder said quietly. He introduced himself and Mattie again, then produced his badge and held it out for a lengthy inspection. "I don't believe I caught your name?" Ryder prompted.

"Paul Linstrum."

"You live here too, Mr. Linstrum?"

He shook his head, smiling faintly. The question seemed to amuse him. "I'm a friend of the family," he said.

"Kind of late to be visting."

"Not necessarily. My place is just two doors down." Staring belligerently, his gray eyes shifted from Ryder to Mattie and then back again, as though he were daring either of them to make something out of the statement.

Linstrum was a head shorter than Ryder but heavier, more solidly built, with thick shoulders, a barrel chest and massive, muscle-corded arms. His face was sun-darkened to a leathery brown and topped by a thatch of thick, pale blond hair that had been carefully combed back in an effort to cover his prominent ears. A jutting chin, deep-set eyes and a small, hard mouth gave him that rugged, ugly-handsome look that some women find attractive. It didn't do anything for Mattie. Very outdoorsy, she decided, but definitely not her type. His overdeveloped body seemed to be straining against the confinement of his plaid shirt and heavy tan cords, the latter held up by one of those belts with the big, ornamental buckles. This one had the legend ''Winchester'' written across the top with the raised profile of a rifle centered below it. Mattie had a sudden but clear picture of him braving the elements in order to blast the crap out of some poor, unsuspecting deer. For no better reason, she immediately disliked him.

''What's it all about?'' Linstrum persisted. ''You just can't come barging in here without an explanation.''

''It's a family matter,'' Ryder said. ''But seeing as you're already here, you might as well stick around.''

''Sure. Why not.'' Linstrum tried to sound indifferent, but couldn't quite bring it off. The lines around his mouth deepened a fraction as though he'd just bitten into something he didn't like the taste of.

Turning abruptly, Mrs. Kendrick led them into a living room decorated in shades of beige and red, a room of soft lights and deep shadows dominated by a fireplace with an antique walnut mantel. There was a fire in the smoke-blackened grate but it wasn't wood they were burning. It was one of those pressed-paper logs, the kind you buy in the supermarket. Mattie watched as the flames ate away the last of the product's familiar bright wrapping.

In spite of the blaze the room had that clean, overly fussy feel to it, an atmosphere that was more like that of a museum than a place where people lived. There was too much furniture

36

for one thing, mostly Victorian and mission-period oak. All of the pieces looked expensive and carefully maintained, but also as though they'd been bought one at a time with no consideration as to how they'd look together. Mattie found the overall effect awkward and unsettling. Costly but not very comfortable.

Picking up a drink from the mantel, Linstrum turned his back on them, his attention seemingly absorbed by the twisting flames of the fire. Mattie had a feeling that, family friend or not, he wasn't going to be much help. Mrs. Kendrick motioned them toward a couch but when she made no move to seat herself, Ryder shook his head.

"Police?" she signed. "An interpreter? I don't understand. Has something happened to Noah?" She looked more confused than apprehensive.

"I'm sorry, Mrs. Kendrick," Ryder began haltingly. He glanced at Mattie to make sure she was signing along. This obviously wasn't something he wanted to go through twice.

"I'm sorry," he repeated, "but I have to inform you that your husband is dead."

With a dull, questioning stare, Ariana Kendrick made the sign for death. Her left hand palm down, her right hand palm up and slightly to the front, she turned them both over. It looked like the phrase it had grown out of . . . "to roll over and die."

She began to cry, paused, drew a ragged breath and rubbed her eyes with the back of her sleeve. When she lowered her arm, a few teardrops still clung stubbornly to her long, feathery lashes.

"How did he die?" she signed. "An accident in the car?" Her fingers manuevered an imaginary steering wheel.

Ryder tugged at his wilting collar. In the stuffy, overheated house his heavy tweed suit must have been about as comfortable as a portable sauna. Still he made no move to shed his jacket or even loosen his tie. Mattie realized it had something to do with respect, the *formality* of death. He really did care. Suddenly, she liked him a whole lot more.

"Your husband was a stabbing victim," Ryder said gently. "A passerby found him near the Thirty-second Street Beach on Lake Calhoun. He was still alive then, but critically wounded. She called an ambulance and he was taken to the County Medical Center, where he died a short while later. I'm truly sorry for your loss." Stumbling over the last few words, Ryder looked down at his shoes.

Ariana Kendrick seemed to shrink, her long body curling inward, closing down on itself. Then she threw her head back and screamed, a piercing, animallike cry of pain that brought up goose bumps along the back of Mattie's neck.

Swearing softly, Mattie reached out and put her arms around the deaf woman. It was unprofessional as hell. She was here as an interpreter and nothing else. But Mattie didn't give a damn. Linstrum certainly wasn't making any move to comfort her. When Mattie glanced up at him, he looked more embarrassed then anything else, like a guest who'd suddenly decided it wasn't his kind of party.

Mattie held tight as the narrow shoulders rose and fell and the screaming faded in muffled sobbing. She began to struggle, pushing against Mattie's arms, thrashing violently in an effort to break free. It was almost as though she were fighting death itself. Damning it for having come into her life. Then, just as suddenly, she went limp, all the strength and tension draining out of her at once. Clumsily, Mattie manuevered Mrs. Kendrick over to the couch where she collapsed. Rolling over, she drew her long legs up in a fetal position and buried her face in a nest of pillows.

For a long moment no one moved, no one spoke a word. Small sounds filled up the silence. The crackle of the fire, Ariana's crying, the rattle of branches on the windowpane, whispery noises that mingled together in an eerie and mournful lamentation for the dead.

5

Linstrum glanced at Mrs. Kendrick, drained his glass and set it carefully on the mantel. "Jesus," he muttered, "it's getting more like New York every day. You can't even walk by the lake after dark without getting mugged."

"It wasn't a mugging," Ryder said quietly. "Kendrick still had his wallet on him when the paramedics brought him in. Cash and credit cards intact. Until there's something to indicate otherwise, we're looking at this as premeditated murder."

Frowning, Linstrum shook his head. "It's got to be some wacko job, a psycho. I can't imagine why anyone would want to kill Noah Kendrick."

"A psycho is one possibility," Ryder admitted, "but it's not the only one." He lowered his bulk into a wing-back chair, then took out a pen and a worn, leather-bound notebook. Mattie sat down too. It felt good to be off her feet. The heat was beginning to make her drowsy. Exciting as this all was, she hoped she wouldn't embarrass herself by falling asleep.

"Can you think of anyone who might want to harm Kendrick?"

Linstrum thought about it for a few seconds, then shook his head. "I honestly can't, Lieutenant. He was a very low-key guy. Kept to himself mostly. Not unfriendly. Just the kind who minded his own business. Maybe it was his deafness that made him like that. It wasn't as though he could talk to the neighbors, even if he wanted to. But he seemed happy enough. He never had any hassles around here. Not that I know of."

"How long have you known the Kendricks?"

"He was living here when I moved into my place, five,

almost six years ago. But I never saw that much of Kendrick until he married Ariana last spring. It's her I know really. She's a lot . . . '' he hesitated, "a lot more social.''

"You know sign language then?''

"A little bit. Ariana's been teaching me.'' By way of a demonstration, he clumsily finger-spelled his name. He might be learning, Mattie thought, but he wasn't working very hard at it.

"Is that what you're here for tonight?''

He shook his head again, a slow grin softening his angular face. "Believe it or not, I'm here to model. Ariana's been working on a portrait of me. She's a very gifted painter.''

Ryder slowly surveyed the room. There were a couple of small oils, western scenes, and a set of four, framed and matted Remington reproductions.

"Those are just things that Noah bought.'' Linstrum made an abrupt, dismissive gesture. "He was a real western history buff. Even wrote about it for some magazines. Ariana's work is more contemporary, more avant-garde. There's some of her paintings upstairs if you want to take a look at them.''

"Maybe later,'' Ryder said. "What time did you arrive here this evening?''

Linstrum frowned, shifting uncomfortably. He obviously hadn't been anticipating the question. "Around five, I guess. Maybe a little before that.''

"Then what did you do?''

"Well, I'd picked up some Chinese takeout on the way over. So we ate, practiced signing for a while, then went out back to Ariana's studio. It's an old gazebo actually. Kendrick had it fixed up for her, thermal windows, baseboard heating, the works. She told me he didn't like the smell the paints made here in the house. Anyway, we were out there all evening. We'd just finished up and had come back to the house a few minutes before you got here.''

"Then you both were either here or out in the studio from five o'clock on?''

40

"That's right." He nodded. "She'll tell you the same thing herself." Turning abruptly, he picked up the fireplace poker and began to prod the crumbling paper log. It split apart with a loud snapping sound, the falling pieces sending up a shower of bright orange sparks.

"What's the nature of your relationship with Mrs. Kendrick?" Ryder asked.

The room seemed to get quieter as Linstrum stiffened and then turned slowly around. His deep-set eyes had narrowed down to slits and his face was flushed, either from anger or the heat of the fire. Beaded sweat clung to his hard-clamped mouth. He was still gripping the heavy-looking poker, hefting it for weight and balance, the way you would a weapon. "What the hell does that mean?" he demanded.

"What it means," Ryder said evenly, "is exactly what I asked you."

Linstrum took a tentative step forward, whacking the poker against his open palm. Meeting the other man's eyes, Ryder remained seated, calm and motionless, as though he were waiting for a bus. Watching the two men, Mattie suddenly wasn't sleepy anymore.

It lasted ten long seconds, a tiny fragment of eternity. Then Linstrum looked away, exhaling audibly as he relaxed his white-knuckled grip on the poker. "We're friends," he said in a low voice. "And that's all there is to it." He mopped his face with a wrinkled handkerchief, then swung round and tossed the poker back in its stand where it landed with a reverberating metallic clatter. "Listen, I won't say that I don't find Ariana attractive, but what the hell. There's a whole town full of them." He grinned at Ryder, man to man. "I'm not the kind of guy who needs to hit on his neighbor's wife." Running his fingers through his thick blond hair, he looked at Mattie as though he expected her to somehow confirm his masculine charms.

Sighing, she closed her eyes. Who did this clown think he was? God's gift to women? She wondered if he was waiting for her to do something, like stand up and cheer. Shifting around, she nestled deeper in the comfortable chair. In the momentary silence, Ariana's muffled sobbing was a strangly soothing counterpoint to the crackle of the fire.

"We really don't have any suspects yet," Ryder said. He sounded tired, mildly disappointed. "Right now we're simply gathering information. As much as we can. We'll sort out what's relevant and what's not as we go along."

Linstrum nodded sympathetically. "I understand, Lieutenant. I only wish there was something more I could tell you." When Mattie opened her eyes again, he was smiling, exuding goodwill as though he'd won some minor but heavily contested point. He reached up and retrieved his empty glass from the mantel. "Can I get you folks a drink?" He'd now assumed the role of genial host.

Ryder shook his head and although she could have used a drink, so did Mattie. She watched as Linstrum crossed the room to where an antique oak cabinet was set against the wall. On top of it there was a brass tray with a cluster of bottles, glassware and a chrome and plastic ice bucket. Linstrum took his time over the refill, especially considering that the end result was nothing more elaborate than a couple of fingers of Jack Daniel's over ice.

"Just a few more questions, Mr. Linstrum." Ryder stretched and then slowly eased himself out of the chair. "Is that your car out in the driveway?"

"The Le Baron? Hardly my style, Lieutenant. I drive a Porsche. The Chrysler out front is Ariana's."

"What about Kendrick?"

"A new Cadillac Seville. Nice, if you like American cars." From the tone of his voice he obviously didn't.

"Do you happen to know if he was driving it tonight?"

Linstrum shrugged. "It's not in the driveway."

"Is there a telephone out in the studio?"

Taking a long pull from his drink, Linstrum swallowed and shook his head. "There's just the two phones here in the house.

One's in the kitchen. The other one's up in the master bedroom. They're both hooked up to TDDs. That's a . . . "

"I know what TDDs are," Ryder cut him short. "But maybe there's something else you can help me with. Before Kendrick died he kept signing a couple of phrases. I think they must have been very important to him. He signed, 'House burned down. No iron man there.' Does that mean anything to you?"

Linstrum moistened his lips and looked down, staring thoughtfully into the amber depths of his drink. "It doesn't ring any bells," he said, looking up again. But there was a flicker of recognition, something there in his pale gray eyes.

"All right. I'll need your address and phone number, in case we need to talk to you again."

"No problem." He reeled them off and Ryder took them down in his notebook. Then he read it back just to make sure.

"Right the first time, Lieutenant. Am I free to go now? I'd like to hang around but it's . . . " Leaving the sentence unfinished, he turned to look at Ariana. The sobbing had stopped without any of them being aware of it. She was curled up on the couch, peacefully asleep, her arms wrapped around her long, denim-clad legs. There was something very childlike about the pose. A frail innocence strangely at odds with her sensuality. It reminded Mattie just how young she really was.

"You're free to go," Ryder told him. "But if you need to leave town for any reason, I'd appreciate you calling me first." He took out his wallet and handed Linstrum one of his cards.

"Does that mean I'm a suspect?"

"It's routine. Nothing personal."

Linstrum nodded, but he still looked unconvinced. His face was tight-set and there was a new wariness in his eyes. Anxiety had deepened the lines around his mouth; beneath the tan his flesh was mottled, infused with a dark drinker's flush. With fumbling fingers he tucked the card in his pocket and then turned and put his drink down on the tray. It was still three-quarters full. But now that Ryder had given him the go-ahead he seemed anxious to be on his way. Mattie knew that he was worried about something. And that something was probably himself.

There was a mirror over the makeshift bar. Linstrum paused in front of it and carefully smoothed back the hair that covered his protruding ears. It was a fussy, almost feminine gesture that didn't fit in with his macho image. As he patted the last stray hairs into place, he spotted Mattie watching him, scowled and turned abruptly away.

Grabbing a sheepskin-lined coat off a nearby chair, he draped it over his massive shoulders, not bothering with the sleeves. He looked at Ryder and smiled. "Call me if you need to, Lieutenant. Goodnight, Miss Shayne." With a casual wave he disappeared into the dimly lit hall. A moment later they heard the heavy door slam behind him.

"A real prince," Ryder said sourly.

"The kind of man who makes celibacy seem like an attractive alternative."

Laughing, Ryder took out his Pall Malls, tapped one free of the mangled pack and lit it. "You know what his biggest problem is?"

"What?"

"He's not a very good liar."

6

Mrs. Kendrick moaned softly. Bracing one arm against the side of the couch, she slowly pulled herself upright. She wasn't completely awake yet. Her heavy-lidded eyes were still fighting the intruding light as she yawned, stretched and then carefully smoothed down her rumpled shirt.

Mattie felt bad about getting her up. But it wasn't her decision and Ryder had been insistent. Watching her now, Mattie felt even worse. Judging from the deaf woman's faint, fuzzy smile, she hadn't remembered yet that the *real* nightmare was still waiting for her on this side of sleep.

She rubbed her eyes and then wiped her hands on her paint-splattered jeans. Her face was red and puffy from crying, the dark hair above it disheveled, with a few stray locks of it sweat-plastered to her damp forehead. Under similar circumstances Mattie would have looked like hell. No jealousy intended, but it bothered her all the more that Ariana Kendrick didn't.

"Are you all right?" Mattie signed. It was a stupid question to ask someone whose husband had just died. But she couldn't think of anything more appropriate.

Ariana blinked, her bleary eyes actually focusing on Mattie for the first time. Her sleepy smile faltered, then died as she realized why Mattie was here, the memory of it taking all the softness out of her face, reshaping it in the stronger, harsher lines of grief. She looked down, took a deep breath and swallowed hard.

"I'm all right," she signed. "I usually don't lose control like that." Forming the words, her hands moved slowly, heav-

45

ily, as though struggling against some new inner gravity. There was a certain stillness about her too. Mattie didn't quite know how to describe it. But it was as though she had stepped inside herself, away from the cold reality of death.

Looking past Mattie's shoulder, she slowly surveyed the room. "Where's Paul?" she signed. She didn't seem upset by his absence. Only curious.

"He had to go," Mattie signed.

Ariana shrugged and Mattie smiled. She wanted to believe that there was nothing between them, that it was a strictly platonic relationship. She liked the woman, although she hadn't yet figured out why. As far as Linstrum was concerned, Mattie felt he was one of those men who could brighten up a room just by leaving it.

"Are you up to answering some questions?" Ryder watched the deaf woman intently while Mattie translated his query into sign.

Ariana nodded eagerly. "Give me a minute, though," she signed. "I'm still a little groggy." Without waiting for Ryder's reply, she leaned back and closed her eyes. It struck Mattie just how well Ariana asserted her control over the situation. Short of their prying her eyes back open, she'd effectively shut down the lines of communication. She was going to answer Ryder's questions, but only when *she* was ready.

Smiling, Mattie glanced at the fire. Ryder was leaning against the mantel, looking disgruntled as he lit up another cigarette. The place was certainly quieter with Linstrum gone. She was aware now of the small creaks and groans that echoed through the house, like murmured phrases from some secret language of the night. The sound of the wind seemed sharper, more clearly defined and from somewhere in the hall, Mattie could hear the soft, synchronized stroke of a pendulum clock. It soothed away some of the anger she felt toward Ryder. But not all of it. He'd set her up. After alluding to Linstrum's lying, Ryder had stubbornly refused to say anything more about it. She still hadn't figured out what Linstrum had been

46

lying about. But what bothered her the most was that Ryder had caught it and she hadn't.

Ariana's eyes flickered open. She sat up and nodded to Ryder, signaling him she was ready to begin. Maybe it was just a trick of the firelight, but Mattie thought she looked calmer, somehow more sure of herself.

"Can you think of anyone who might have wanted to harm your husband? Anyone he quarreled with recently?" Mattie translated the question into sign. His eyes intent on the deaf woman's face, Ryder thumbed open a fresh page in his notebook.

Frowning throughtfully, Ariana shook her head. "He was a kind man . . . very gentle." She dragged one open palm across the other. It was the sign for "nice," also for "clean." Then she finger-spelled "gentle," in an effort to be more precise. In ASL, there was no specific sign for the word.

"Noah didn't have any enemies," she continued. "There was no *reason* for anyone to want to kill him." She bit her lower lip and gazed into the fire. Her sharp features settled into a troubled yet intense expression, as though she were close to something but it was still, inexplicably, beyond her grasp.

"Private," she signed finally. "He was a very private man. He had his business, our life, friends, his books and writing. Nothing else. He didn't need anything else." She looked bewildered over the last part. Mattie sensed that it was as much a question as a statement. A question that Ariana hadn't yet been able to answer herself.

Ryder shifted restlessly. The clock in the hallway sounded the hour. It was getting late. "When was the last time you saw him?" Ryder asked.

"This morning at breakfast."

"Did anything unusual occur? Did he seem worried, different in any way?"

After a moment's consideration, Ariana made a brief, dismissive gesture. "He was the same as always," she signed. "A little preoccupied . . . anxious to get to work. But that

47

wasn't unusual. He loved his work. It was the biggest part of what he was . . . of what he always wanted to be.'' She paused and rubbed her eyes with the back of her hand and then slowly surveyed the expensively furnished living room as though she wanted to remind them, and herself, just how successful Kendrick had been.

Ryder tapped his notebook. "Do you know what his plans were for this evening?"

She nodded eagerly. "Fridays were special, a kind of tradition. Noah and a friend of his, Todd Meredith, always met after work for dinner and a few games of chess. Todd is deaf too. He and his wife run the Sunset Gallery. They specialize in western art.'' Using her fingertips as a brush, she drew them back and forth across her open palm like an artist slapping paint on a canvas. She tipped her head toward the Remington prints on the wall. "Not my kind of thing,'' she signed. "It was boys' night out, anyway. They never invited me or Mara, Todd's wife, to come along.'' Leaning back, she ran her fingers through her close-cropped hair. The faintest of smiles softened her face for a second, but it died before it reached her dark, somber eyes.

"Where's the gallery located?"

"I don't know the address, but it's on Hennepin near Thirty-first.''

Ryder shot Mattie a meaningful glance. But when their eyes met he quickly lowered his head, suddenly absorbed in his notebook. She didn't *know* what he was thinking, but she could hazard a pretty good guess: That the gallery was only a few blocks away from the deserted stretch of Lake Calhoun shoreline where Kendrick had been dumped. Was it just a coincidence? Somehow, Mattie didn't think so.

"All right.'' Ryder looked up again and sighed. "When did you expect your husband home tonight?"

"Around ten,'' Ariana signed. She paused for a second, her slender hands trembling. "When I saw your headlights,'' she continued, "I thought it might be Noah. But it turned out I was mistaken." Mattie thought she was going to start crying again. But instead, the deaf woman's mouth curved upward in a bitter smile. Silently, she seemed to be saying that life had played some obscene and undeserved joke on her. And there wasn't anything anyone could do about it.

Mattie made a small noise in her throat. She was halfway out of her chair before Ryder's glaring, angry eyes forced her back again. She wished she could offer the woman some comfort, do *something* for her. But this obviously wasn't the time or place. More important, she reminded herself, it wasn't why Ryder had brought her along. Mattie took a deep breath, trying to ignore the blush she felt mounting her cheeks.

Ryder thumbed open a fresh page in his notebook, his gaze shifting to Ariana. "What did you do this evening?" he asked softly.

"I was with Paul," she signed quickly. Almost *too* quickly, Mattie thought as she voiced the reply for Ryder. She noticed something else as well, a new guarded wariness in the depths of Ariana's red-rimmed eyes. "He brought over some food," she went on, "then we ate and went out to the studio." Turning, she gestured vaguely toward the rear of the house. "I painted all evening. When we were done we came back to the house. That was only a few minutes before you arrived." She stopped signing but her watchful gaze lingered on Mattie, almost as though she were daring her to contradict her.

"Was Linstrum with you all the time?" Ryder asked.

Ariana nodded, not bothering to raise her hands from her lap. Her fingers absently toyed with her thick gold wedding band as though, subconciously, she were deciding whether she should keep it on or not.

"Let me get this straight," Ryder said irritably. "You spent most of this evening in the studio out back. You didn't walk or drive anywhere else?"

Mattie translated the question and the deaf woman nodded eagerly. Again her harsh but beautiful face held an expression that was almost blatantly defiant. Mattie wondered what she was trying to prove? That in spite of all the time she spent alone with Linstrum, their relationship was as innocent as he'd described it? Or did that look mean just the opposite? She honestly couldn't tell. Frustrated, Mattie gave up trying to figure it out. "What kind of car did your husband drive?"

"A Cadillac Seville," Ariana signed, her fingers quickly spelling out the letters that formed the name. "It's black," she added. "This year's model. I take it you haven't found it yet?"

Ryder shook his head. "I'm sure we will. It would help if you had the license number and registration?"

Ariana slipped off the couch and crossed the room to where a small, cherrywood desk rested against the back wall. Mattie was surprised at the change in her carriage, the way she walked. She seemed suddenly graceless in her grief. Her head bowed, her shoulders stiff with tension, she moved with the shambling gait of someone recovering from a long illness, as though the strings that had held her taut and erect had been cut away and left to dangle.

"A broken doll," Mattie muttered and immediately hated herself for saying it. It was a lousy analogy and hardly in the best interests of feminism, but it was exactly what Ariana reminded her of.

She carried a red leather-bound address book over to Ryder and tapped the open page with her forefinger. He copied the information down, closed the book and returned it with a solemn nod of thanks.

"One other thing," he said looking up at her. "Your husband kept signing something before he died. 'House burned down . . . No iron man there.' Does it meaning anything to you?"

To Mattie's surprise, Ariana nodded eagerly. "We had a cabin up north," she signed. "Near Lake Vermilion. It burned down last April. The local authorities suspected arson, but they were never able to find out who did it. I'm sure that must be what Noah meant. But I don't understand why he thought it was so important." She looked confused now and, somehow, vaguely disappointed.

50

"What about the iron man?"

"Nothing." Her slender hands fluttered nervously, as though she were afraid of letting him down. "It doesn't mean anything to me." Her face was flushed from the heat. Or maybe, Mattie thought, from the lie she'd just told. Mattie's job was reading people and although the change was to subtle to pinpoint, she was sure the deaf woman wasn't telling the truth.

Ryder snapped his notebook shut. "I'll need a picture of your husband. A recent one, taken in sunlight, if you have it." He paused and took a deep breath. "I know this is a difficult time for you, but we need to make arrangements for you to identify the . . ."

Suddenly Ryder bolted out of his chair, discarded notebook and pen tumbling to the floor. He ran through the archway and down the hall, feet pounding against the bare wood. The front door crashed open with a thunderous, echoing sound like a gunshot.

The noise slowly died as the cold, wet wind rushed in to fill the house.

7

Ariana's mouth went slack. Her dark eyes widened with puzzlement then fear. "It's all right," Mattie signed quickly. "There's someone outside."

Mattie knew what had jolted him out of his seat. She'd heard it herself, a sudden loud snapping sound that had nothing to do with the night or the wind. She hurried to the front window with Ariana in her wake and peered out into the darkness, her stomach knotted up in a cold rush of fear.

There's nothing to be afraid of, she reminded herself. But she felt vulnerable and foolish at the same time. Someone *had* been lurking out there, crouching outside the window. The murderer? It was a stupid move on his part, but whoever said Noah Kendrick's killer had to be smart? She'd seen Kendrick dying, seen the obscene cross-hatching of knife wounds cut into his chest. She never wanted to get anywhere near someone who could do that to another human being.

Ariana had her nose pressed against the glass. There wasn't much to see though. The lawn was a patchwork of shadow and moonlight, the street beyond it empty and quiet. They watched Ryder as he ran across the grass, his tie loose and flapping out behind him like the tail of an earthbound kite.

He disappeared into the darkness, suddenly swallowed up by the ebon night. For a few seconds more Mattie could hear him running, heavy shoes slapping the blacktopped street. When the sounds of his footfalls faded away, there was nothing left to listen to but the angry thrash and pull of the wind.

Turning, Mattie glanced at Ariana. Her face was still brushing the misted windowpane, as though touching the glass would help her to "hear," to connect with some bit of reality she didn't understand. Her full lips were moving, mouthing something Mattie couldn't make out. She didn't look frightened. She looked terrified.

Mattie wondered if she should phone for help. "Backup." That's what the police called it. It was probably too soon for that but she thought she should close the front door. Better yet, *lock* it. She started to turn away and then stopped, hesitating, suddenly indecisive. There might or might not be a murderer running loose out there, but she *knew* that Ryder was somewhere in the cold darkness. She was sure he could take care of himself. But what if he . . .

He stepped suddenly out of the shadows, his broad back outlined by the white vapor wash of a street lamp. He was poised, listening now, straining to hear the slightest sound. Mattie could almost feel his intensity. He'd drawn his gun and was holding it, barrel upright, lamp light gleaming off the shiny, blued steel.

He put the gun away, turned and walked slowly back, hands thrust deep in his pockets, his head slightly bowed. He looked dejected and Mattie felt a sudden wave of sympathy. They'd both had a long, hard night, but police work must be full of them. Long nights and plenty of disappointment too.

Beside her, Ariana bit her lip, anxiety flickering in her black eyes like the flash of a distant signal light. Mattie reached out to put her hand on her shoulder, but the deaf woman turned on her heel and strode over to the makeshift bar. Peering intently at the array of bottles, she sighed and hefted a liter of off-brand vodka. Her hands were shaking; the neck of the bottle chattered against the glass, the hollow clatter sounding like a few bars of bad experimental music.

Mattie took two steps in her direction and then stopped abruptly. Did Ryder expect her to keep Ariana out of the booze? Probably. A stiff drink on top of the shock she'd had could render her pretty well useless for any further interrogation. Mattie decided she didn't give a damn. She was too tired, and not self-righteous enough, to try and wrestle a glass away from a grieving widow.

"I lost him," Ryder announced. He took a few shuffling steps into the living room and then halted, his heavy body sagging against the archway. "Almost nailed him," he gasped, "but the son of a bitch outran me. Had too much of a head start."

Mattie nodded sympathetically. Ryder was breathing heavily, the exhaled air whistling through his clenched teeth. Above the trim line of his beard, his cheeks were mottled with dark, purplish color and his barrel chest rose and fell as though he'd just run a marathon instead of half a block. Diplomacy had never been one of Mattie's strong suits, but something bright and burning in Ryder's eyes stopped her from saying anything about his smoking. If there ever was a time for it, this *wasn't* it.

"Did you get a good look at him?" she asked.

"Too dark. But it was a *him*, I'm pretty sure of that. His silhouette . . . the way he ran." Sighing, he took out his Pall Malls and shook one free of the crumpled pack. He had trouble getting a match going and when he finally did, it trembled slightly in his oversize hands, the cigarette above it dancing and bobbing before it finally connected with the flame. Mattie quickly looked away, realizing for the first time that Ryder had been scared out there alone in the dark. He seemed embarrassed to show it, but Mattie understood. Her brother, Wes, had told her a little bit about Vietnam, about the adrenalin rush of combat and then the aftermath when suddenly you'd be shaking all over, a scared-shitless eighteen-year-old again.

"It's getting late," Ryder said softly. "Just give me a few more minutes of your time and we'll call it a night." His tone was almost apologetic. "I'll drive you home . . . hell of a long one . . . know you must be tired." He was talking too much now, suddenly anxious to fill up the uncomfortable silence between them with meaningless words.

"No problem," Mattie assured him. She didn't know what

55

else to say. When she turned back around, he avoided her eyes as though he'd seen something in them, something that told him too much about himself.

It took them another half hour to wrap it up. During all that time Ryder never once looked at Mattie directly.

Along with a brief list of friends and business associates, Ariana produced an eight-by-ten of Kendrick, smiling, relaxed and confident as he posed in front of the cabin that was now, presumably, a fire-gutted ruin. She asked about claiming her husband's body and through Mattie, Ryder haltingly explained that she would have to make a formal identification first and that the remains couldn't be released until after an autopsy had been completed.

Reminding Ariana of the intruder outside her window, Ryder offered her police protection, which she politely but firmly refused. Frustrated but still trying, Ryder suggested that she check into a hotel for the night or else make arrangements with a friend to sleep over. But Ariana remained adamant; whatever her reasons were, she was determined to stay in the big, old house alone. In the end there was nothing Ryder and Mattie could do but leave.

When the door closed behind them, Ryder paused on the porch to hitch up his jacket collar against the icy blast. "Like a steam bath in there," he muttered. "Wonder why they keep it so hot? Must cost them a small fortune."

"Maybe one of them grew up *cold*. It's something that stays with you." She wasn't talking about her own childhood, which had been comfortably, almost boringly middle class. But one of the clearest memories of her misspent youth was the night she'd slept over at her friend Amy's house. She couldn't have been more than eight or nine at the time. But she could still remember shivering under the heaped-on, musty-smelling covers, the *weight* of the freezing cold air pressing down on her. And more than anything, the feeling, deep down inside her, that she'd never be warm again.

"Interesting theory," Ryder commented, but his tone of voice said it was anything but.

56

"It's a possibility," Mattie insisted. "And don't try to humor me. We're both too tired for that." She jammed her hands in the pockets of her trench coat and continued walking, her heavy feet crunching their way through the brittle, wind-driven leaves. "You really don't know anything about their backgrounds. Might be worth checking out."

Lumbering along beside her, Ryder nodded silently. He was, Mattie decided, either being polite or trying to ignore her. Since she probably wouldn't see him again, it really didn't matter. Still, she was curious about the Kendricks, where they had come from, what their lives had been like *before* the stately house in Kenwood, the immaculate gardener-tended lawn, the new Cadillac Seville? She couldn't quite put her finger on it, but there was something almost haunted about the overheated, over-furnished living room, as if the excess of warmth and luxury somehow kept at bay the memory ghosts of a hand-to-mouth past.

When they reached the cruiser, Ryder's cold hands fumbled with the keys. Swearing softly, he unlocked the passenger door for Mattie first and then turned to walk around to the other side. She reached out impulsively and grabbed his arm, forcing him to turn back and look at her. "Are you going to tell me what Linstrum was lying about?" she demanded. "You don't have to, but if you're not, I wish you wouldn't have mentioned it. It just isn't fair."

For a couple of seconds Ryder studied her silently, his broad face thoughtful in the pale glow of the sedan's interior light. "All right," he said finally, "but you'll have to keep it to yourself." Mattie nodded. Who did he think she was going to tell?

"It wasn't just Linstrum," Ryder said. "Both of them were lying." His voice was thick with anger now. "Remember when we got here? On the way up to the house, we stopped for a minute to look at the car?"

Nodding again, Mattie's gaze drifted past him to where the gleaming Le Baron was parked. "Well," Ryder continued,

57

"when we walked past, I just happened to run my hand over the hood. I wasn't checking, it was just . . . reflex action, something you do without even thinking about it. Now I'm damn glad I did it because the engine was still *warm*. It's her car and it's locked up tight, so that pretty well eliminates some kids having taken it for a joy ride. The way I figure it, the grieving widow and Linstrum got there just a few minutes before we did. Anyway," he sighed, "they sure as hell didn't spend the whole night out in the gazebo making art."

Mattie took a deep breath. "Then that means . . . "

"That neither one of their alibis is worth a damn. I don't know what they're trying to cover up, but I'm going to find out. Right now, as far as I'm concerned, either one of them could have murdered the old man."

Shivering, Mattie brushed her wind-whipped hair back from her face. "Is that why you offered her police protection? You *wanted* someone around to keep an eye on her."

"Partly. But mostly for her protection. Don't look now, but there's an unmarked blue Chevy parked across from the next house down. I stopped to use the car radio on my way back from my late-night sprint. So if she decides to go anywhere else tonight, she's going to have some company."

It took Mattie a long time to get to sleep. She woke up twice in the dead, quiet hours before dawn, her skin slippery with sweat, her long legs tangled in the bedclothes. The dream had been exactly the same both times. She was in a cold, deserted graveyard. Overhead the moon hung, orange and bloated in a polished ebon sky without stars.

Surrounded by a jumble of crooked tombstones, she was kneeling down in front of a mound of dark, fresh-turned earth. Protruding out of it were dozens of hands, their fingers daubed with blood and smeared with the damp, clinging dirt. The hands never stopped moving. Jerking wildly, out of control, they kept making signs. Signs that Mattie couldn't read.

8

Mattie woke to the sound of rain on the roof. Huddling under the covers she listened to the hard, insistent drumming overhead and the smaller accompanying noises, the swish of tires on the pavement below, the rattle of loose weather stripping, the soft gurgle of rainwater as it tried to push its way through the rusty, leaf-choked gutters. She felt like pulling the comforter over her head, shutting out all the rain sounds, not getting up until the sun came out. Instead, she kicked the bedclothes off, swung her long legs over the side and padded barefoot to the window overlooking the street.

It framed a picture that was soft and diffused, almost impressionistic, but only if the Impressionists had been heavily into depression. Even the brightest colors were washed out and rendered in shades of muted gray; all the sharp lines and angles were lost, turned misty-edged and wavering by the rain.

Muttering to herself, she turned away and stumbled toward the bathroom. Some twenty minutes later she was showered and dressed, comfortable if not elegant in a heavy cotton sweater and her favorite old jeans. She went downstairs, through the dark and quiet house, pausing along the way to switch on lamps that didn't quite manage to dispel the gloom of the storm.

In the kitchen she turned on more lights and got the Proctor-Silex going. Leaning against the refrigerator, she closed her eyes again, shutting out everything for a moment, savoring the perfect peacefulness of a lazy Saturday morning. The smell of fresh-brewed coffee slowly filled the room. The bubble and hiss of the machine was comforting, normal, a small part of the "regular world," untouched by violence or sudden death.

At the kitchen table Mattie sipped her coffee and thought about the night before. She was worried about Ariana Kendrick. Why had she lied to them? What was she trying to cover up? An affair with Linstrum? Somehow it just didn't seem right. Affairs had become a sad but permanent part of the marital landscape these days, something that *happened* whether you wanted them to or not. She knew *that* well enough, from bitter, personal experience. And Kendrick had been so much older. But in a murder investigation it was a stupid motive for lying. And Ariana Kendrick didn't strike her as a stupid person.

Maybe Mattie had read her wrong. But she didn't think so. She wished she could talk to her alone, woman to woman. She had a feeling that Ariana would open up without Ryder there peering over her shoulder. But if he ever found out . . . Mattie didn't even want to think about that.

She finished her coffee and got up for a refill, pausing along the way to turn the radio on. Her hand on the dial, she glanced out the kitchen window and froze. There was someone out there. Someone watching the house from the alleyway that ran behind the garage. She took a slow, deep breath and peered out the rain-blurred window.

The figure suddenly spun round and vanished into the rain, leaving Mattie with a vague impression of height and a glistening, hooded black rain poncho. She couldn't tell if it had been a man or a woman, a neighbor on an innocent errand or a stranger just passing by. Still, she couldn't shake the sensation that someone had been *watching* her. But why? All she'd done was interpret Kendrick's dying words; she was only a translator with no real part in the investigation. Why would a stranger be watching her house?

Shivering, Mattie turned away from the window. A second later she heard the sputter and grind of a car starting up in the alley. The engine caught on the second try and the unseen car sped away, its tires machine-gunning gravel as it raced down the narrow, rutted access road. After it was gone Mattie stood still, listening. But there was nothing out there now but the relentless pounding of the rain.

60

She was checking the lock on the front door when the phone rang. Her hands were shaking and she had to stop and steady them before she lifted the receiver.

"Hello," she said cautiously.

"Good morning, Miss Shayne." There was a brief pause. "This is Lieutenant Ryder."

Mattie thought she'd recognized the voice at the first words, but she hadn't been completely sure until he'd identified himself. She felt the tension of the last few minutes beginning to slip away.

"Morning, Lieutenant. Is this a social call or was there something I could do for you?"

On the other end of the line she heard a deep sigh. "To be entirely up front about it," Ryder said, "I need your help."

"That wasn't so hard, Lieutenant."

"Maybe not," he muttered, "but then you didn't have to say it."

Mattie laughed, enjoying the sudden feeling of release. With the gloomy stormbound house and the "watcher" lurking in the alleyway, talking to someone with a sense of humor was exactly what she needed.

"Anyway," Ryder continued, "if you're free I'd like you to work with me for a few more days. It shouldn't be too hard and the pay is the same as last night. But it might," he hesitated, "it might take them a while to get you a check."

"No problem," she said grinning to herself. She'd done government work before. It *always* took them a while to get you a check. "Why me?" she asked abruptly.

"Well, I could get a police interpreter. But they'd be coming into this cold. You, on the other hand, were with Kendrick when he died. You already know the widow. And that's important, because I'm probably going to have to question her again. I've also got to talk to that other deaf man, Todd Meredith, the one who owns the gallery where Kendrick was supposed to go last night. So you could really help me out here. I'll probably only need you for a couple of hours, but I'll see that you're paid for the whole day. You can ride with me. You won't even need to use your car."

"I've got school on Monday," she reminded him.

"Just give me these two days."

Ryder's voice was deep, resonant with sincerity. If Mattie hadn't known him already, she would have mistaken him for a vacuum cleaner salesman closing in for the kill. But it seemed as though he really did want and need her help.

"All right," she said finally. "But only if you tell me what's going on. Not just my part of it, but the whole investigation."

There was a long moment of silence on the other end of the line. "Okay," Ryder sighed. "You got yourself a deal. As long as you promise not to go Nancy Drew on me, I'll tell you everything I can. Fair enough?"

"Fair enough. When do you need me?"

"Now."

"I'll be ready in fifteen minutes."

"I'll be there in twenty. 'Bye." The line went dead. Smiling to herself, Mattie gently cradled the receiver.

She had one last cup of coffee, shut the machine off and checked the locks on all the windows, upstairs and down. She felt safer knowing that Ryder was on the way over, but she still wanted the house to be as difficult to break into as she could make it. The lurking figure in the black poncho had frightened her more than she wanted to admit. She *was* involved in a homicide investigation, if only peripherally. In those circumstances someone watching her house was something she just couldn't brush aside, ignore. She'd tell Ryder about it. But there really wasn't anything he could do. Unless there'd been a recent change in the law, looking at her place of residence wasn't a criminal act yet. Just bad manners, or worse. Maybe a whole lot worse.

A few minutes before Ryder was due to arrive, Mattie tugged on a pair of canvas and rubber paddock boots and got her trench coat and an old "Stockman" model Stetson out of the hall closet. Dressed for the weather now, she sat at the bottom of the staircase and waited, eyes half-closed as she listened to the rain.

At the sound of tires clawing for purchase on the wet gravel, Mattie got up and peered out the rain-streaked window. It was Ryder; even in this downpour his bearded, thick-shouldered presence was unmistakable. He waved at her but made no move to get out of the car.

Mattie waved back and after double locking the front door behind her, she sprinted for the car, enjoying the fresh feel of the wind-driven rain on her face.

"Like your hat," Ryder said grinning.

"It was my Uncle Red's. You'd probably like him, too. He swears a lot."

Ryder nodded. "Sounds like a regular guy." He turned his attention back to driving, backing smoothly out of the drive and down Irving Avenue. He had the sedan's heater on low; the warm, trapped air was thick with the smell of tobacco smoke. The car's wipers made a comforting, whispery sound as they swept the beaded moisture off the windshield. There was something, Mattie decided, very secure about a cop car.

"We're going over to the gallery first," Ryder said. "That's where Kendrick was headed last night. It's the logical place to start."

"Any new developments?"

"A few," Ryder said sighing. "I haven't forgotten our deal. Mrs. Kendrick identified the body this morning. No surprises there. We used a departmental interpreter on that one. From what you said last night, I figured you wanted to sleep in."

"Thanks. Is that it?"

Ryder shook his head. "Kiefer and a couple of uniforms worked the Kendricks' neighborhood this morning. They found two witnesses who saw the widow and Linstrum last night, leaving the house together in her car, the Le Baron. Both witnesses place the time somewhere between five and a quarter to. So now we *know* they're lying. All that I need is someone to lock down the time when they got *back*."

"I still don't think she did it," Mattie said quietly.

"Why?"

"Just instinct, I don't think she's capable of committing murder, especially her husband's. I know it isn't logical. But I've always been quick to judge people, to *read* them, and I'm almost always right. It's a trait I have in common with a lot of my deaf friends. If you can't hear, you have to rely on your gut reaction. Sometimes that's all you've got to go on."

To Mattie's surprise, Ryder nodded agreement. "It's the same way with me," he said. "In fact, I don't know a single good cop who doesn't rely on his instincts."

"Then you don't think she did it either?"

He shrugged. "Maybe yes, maybe no. The problem is she's the *only* suspect I've got right now and that fairy story she spun us last night isn't helping her at all." He lit a cigarette off the dashboard lighter and cracked his window a quarter of an inch, blowing a spiral of smoke out at the rain. "Murders are a lot like accidents," he said in a voice that was soft, almost apologetic. "Most of them happen close to home. For your sake I hope I'm wrong. But right now her alibi stinks so bad it should have it's own drawer at the morgue."

Mattie turned and stared out at the rain. They were three or four blocks from Calhoun Square now. The gallery should be somewhere up in the next block; she had a vague memory of having gone in there once to look at something she liked but couldn't possibly afford. Ryder had slowed the sedan to a crawl as he searched for a parking place.

"Something happened this morning," she said. Calmly, she told Ryder about the intruder in the alley and the sound of the car taking off after she'd spotted him. "Maybe it isn't anything," she concluded, "but I thought I'd better tell you about it."

"Damn right," Ryder muttered. "You can never be too careful." He leaned forward and ground out his butt in the ashtray. "For your own good," he said hesitantly, "I think you should stop helping me with the investigation."

64

Mattie shook her head. "I appreciate your concern, Lieutenant, but I don't think it would help. If somebody *is* watching me it's already too late."

"Yeah, you're probably right." He sighed and rubbed his heavy, bearded jaw. "Maybe you should move in with a friend for a while. Just till we wrap this up."

"Absolutely not. I just moved *into* the damn house two months ago. I'm not going to let some jerk in a poncho scare me away."

Spotting a parking place, Ryder goosed the sedan, shooting forward half a block and then carefully angling back into the opening. "I can have the patrol cars check your place periodically," he continued. "But with the caseload we've got, I just don't have enough bodies to assign someone to you full time."

Mattie smiled. "Let's not get carried away, Lieutenant. Maybe it's just a secret admirer."

"Damn it, you *need* some protection. I know a private investigator, a woman . . ."

"I have a gun," she said abruptly. "A .45 Army automatic."

His blue eyes narrowed as he jerked his head around to stare at her. "Registered?"

"Yes."

"Know how to use it?"

Mattie nodded. "My Uncle Red taught me."

"I should have guessed. He seems to be a major influence in your life."

Mattie grinned as she thought about that long, hot August afternoon. She was fifteen and the family had been on the way up to the Boundary Waters for a vacation. They'd stopped to see Red and his second wife, Charlene, who were living in a trailer park near Bemidji. After the brief social ammenities, Uncle Red took his Army .45 and a sack full of Grain Belt empties and the two of them snuck off to a nearby ravine where he taught her, patiently and carefully, how to use the gun.

When her mother found out she threw a shit fit. Not that that changed anything. Later, on her twenty-first birthday, Uncle Red gave her the gun. It was the same one he'd brought back from France after the war.

Mattie turned and looked at Ryder. "He taught me how to use it," she said, "but he told me he hoped I'd never have to."

"This Uncle Red of yours, he live in the Cities?"

"No, he's down in Shakopee now."

"Let me know if he comes to town."

"Why?"

"I want to buy him a drink."

9

The short, heavyset man smiled shyly at Mattie. "You folks must be *real* art lovers," he said. "Nobody else crazy enough to come out on a day like this. Even the critics stayed home, which is where most of them belong, anyway."

Mattie returned the smile. "Actually, I am an art lover. But we're here . . ."

"Police," Ryder said quietly. He reached for the leather folder in his hip pocket, flipped it open and held it out. Under the gallery's soft, recessed lighting the gold shield glowed like freshly polished brass work.

The short man nodded. "Right. Of course. You're here about Noah." He stared at the badge for a few more seconds, critically, appraisingly. For a moment Mattie thought he might make Ryder an offer on it.

"I'm Todd Meredith, the owner of the gallery." He thrust out a soft-looking, pinkish hand and shook Ryder's and then Mattie's with a grave, almost old world formality. "Hell of a thing about Noah. Brutal, absolutely senseless. Ariana called me this morning. At first I couldn't believe it. If there's *anything* I can do to help just tell me what it is."

Ryder looked confused, momentarily caught off balance. "Miss Shayne isn't a police officer," he explained. "She's an interpreter working with me on . . . "

"I should have guessed," Meredith said, a slow, soft smile pulling up the corners of his mouth. "I *am* deaf, though obviously not what you expected, Lieutenant. I can hear some loud noises, pick up some vibrations. I *can't* hear you but I happen to be an excellent lip reader."

He peered up at Ryder, bright green eyes narrowing slightly. "It's the beard and mustache. They tend to mask the movements your mouth makes to form the words. But it's not a problem. I can still understand you." He was rattling on, trying to ease Ryder's discomfort. His plump, flushed face was sympathetic, as though he somehow shared Ryder's embarrassment.

Ryder cleared his throat. "Nice place you've got here."

"Thank you, Lieutenant. I'm moderately successful. Although I wouldn't be able to run it without my wife, Mara. She is hearing, and handles all the phoning, which is quite a lot. But I put this place together myself." He paused and tapped his sagging chest with a blunt forefinger, wrinkling the fabric of his bright yellow sweater. "I'm proud of that. I think it's good for people to see a deaf man with his own art gallery. It negates the myth of *dependency*. Too many people think of the deaf as charity cases. You've seen those cheap little hustlers who pass out cards on buses, the ones with the manual alphabet printed on them. Did you ever try signing to them? Most of them don't even *have* a hearing loss. They're just working a con, manipulating people's sympathy for spare change."

"I never knew that," Ryder said. He sounded genuinely surprised. "But now that I do, I'll keep my money in my pocket next time."

"I'm sorry," Meredith mumbled. He shook his head; Mattie could tell he was embarrassed. "You didn't come here to talk about *me* or deafness. Why don't we sit down? Whatever questions you have, I'll try to answer them as best I can."

Without waiting for a reply, he turned and led them toward the rear of the gallery where four low, comfortable-looking chairs were positioned around a glass-topped table. Walking alongside him, Mattie noticed his small, behind-the-ear hearing aid, only partly concealed by his thinning, sand-colored hair. She guessed he was somewhere in his early forties, but his pudgy, boyish face made it hard to tell for sure. He was dressed in typical uptown sloppy-chic—wrinkled hundred-dollar cords,

68

loafers, and, of course, the sweater that was the same pulsing, bright yellow as a traffic sign.

When they were seated Ryder said, "Tell me about last night."

"Well, there's not all that much to tell. Noah must have been on his way here when it happened. I'm sure Ariana told you that Noah and I had a long-standing date, chess and dinner every Friday evening. It *must* have happened on his way here," Meredith repeated insistently. He shifted his gaze to Mattie. She saw that his eyes had a vacant, almost haunted looked to them. A look of death remembered.

"I know it's stupid," he said slowly. "But I can't help feeling responsible in some way. If he hadn't been on his way to see me, he might still be alive." His voice cracked a little as he stumbled over the last few words. He jammed his hands in the pockets of his wrinkled cords and looked down, focusing on the toes of his scuffed brown loafers.

"Did you have any contact at all with him yesterday?" Ryder asked. After a couple of seconds of silence passed, he frowned.

"Tap him on the shoulder," Mattie whispered. "He didn't *see* you talking."

Ryder nodded and reaching out, put his hand on Meredith's shoulder. The deaf man looked up, vaguely startled, the bright green eyes finally meeting Ryder's. "I'm sorry," he said softly. "I'm not dealing with this very well. I don't have many friends, not close ones at least. It's hard to believe I'm never going to see Noah again."

"I understand," Ryder said sympathetically. "Did you see him yesterday, have any contact with him at all?"

Meredith shook his head. "No reason to, really. He always comes by the gallery to meet me. Usually between five and five-thirty. It's after closing time but if you ring the bell by the door it triggers a flashing light back in my office. Anyway, I was out front here from five o'clock on. If he'd shown up, I would have seen him." Frowning, he rubbed his plump hands together as though he were trying to stimulate circulation. The gallery was comfortable, maybe even a little too warm. But watching Meredith, Mattie again got the impression of someone fighting off the cold.

Ryder was writing in his notebook. Mattie hadn't seen him take it out but there it was, opened to a fresh page and balanced on his knee.

Looking up again, he said, "Were you here alone?"

"Only for a few minutes. Mara left around four-thirty. We weren't busy and she knew I was expecting Noah. But shortly after she took off, Neil Travers, one of the artists we represent, came by. We talked about his upcoming show while I waited for Noah to show up. Of course, he never did." His voice dropped a little, slurring the last few words, almost as though he didn't want to say them.

"Where could I contact Mister Travers?"

"I'll write down his address and number for you," Meredith said. He slipped a business card out of a silver pocket case and wrote on the back of it with a chunky, black and gold Monte Blanc. After fanning the ink dry, he handed the card to Ryder.

"That's his studio. He has a small apartment above it. The phone number's the same for both."

Nodding, Ryder tucked the card in the back of his notebook. "About last night," he continued. "When Kendrick didn't show up, weren't you a little concerned, worried?"

Meredith hesitated. "Yes and no, Lieutenant. This isn't the first time Noah missed one of our Fridays without letting me know. To be frank, these things are harder when you're deaf. You can't just pick up a phone to cancel an engagement. If your car breaks down or you're stuck in traffic . . . if you're anywhere where there *isn't* a TDD, you're out of luck."

"So you weren't particularly worried then?"

"No, not really."

"Did you try to contact him?"

"Yes. At six and again at six-thirty. No one answered.

70

When I mentioned it to Ariana this morning, she said she'd been out back in her studio all evening.''

Ryder glanced at Mattie but didn't say anything. He obviously didn't intend to say anything about Ariana's "alibi."

Meredith folded his hands and stared down at his reflection in the shiny glass tabletop. "Maybe I should have gone by his house last night, phoned him again or *something*. But I've been incredibly preoccupied with this new show. It's something very special. The pieces on the back wall are all genuine Russells. Charles Marion Russell.'' He said the name softly, almost reverently. "He was the best, the only true cowboy artist of his time. Those paintings were the acquisition of a lifetime.'' He shrugged, his smile widening to expose small, even teeth. "But then that's what I'm in business for.''

"They're beautiful,'' Ryder said dutifully. He sounded as though his mind was on something other than art.

Mattie angled her head to look at the paintings. She'd been focusing on Todd Meredith since they arrived; she'd been only vaguely aware of her surroundings and the art on display. The four Russells truly were magnificent, raw bright canvases of tremendous energy and power, alive with an inner fire contrasted and contained by the warm, cream-colored walls that surrounded them. There were other works on the adjoining walls—sketches, oils and watercolors. There was a bronze bison and a bronco rider, each on its own white pedestal. But nothing she saw had the impact, the sheer grandeur of the Russells.

At the sound of the street door, they all turned to watch a man emerge from the rain. He had to duck a bit to keep from denting the crown of his weather-stained gray Stetson. The face beneath it was long and lantern-jawed, hard knobs of bone covered by sun-darkened skin as wrinkled and seamed as old rawhide. He moved with a slow, easy grace, broad shoulders straining the fabric of his faded denim jacket, his stacked-heel western boots digging into the rug.

His dark eyes locked on Mattie. They were deep-set beneath

a bony ridge of brow and surrounded by crow's feet and pouched, wrinkled skin. As he approached, Mattie noticed the stubby butt end of a handmade cigarette dangling from the corner of his mouth.

"Nothing like a pretty lady to pick up a rainy day," he said tipping his hat to her. His voice was soft-pitched, slow but steady, like water brushing over river rocks.

Mattie grinned. "That's the nicest compliment I've had all week. Come to think of it, it's probably the only one."

"Hard to believe," he said, shaking his head. "I'm gonna have to have a talk with your friend here." His dark, steady gaze swung over to Ryder while a slow grin rearranged the wrinkled lines of his face. The cigarette butt clung stubbornly to his lower lip, sending up little puffs of smoke like an Indian signal fire.

"Neil Travers," he said thrusting out a gnarled hand for Ryder to shake.

"We were just talking about you," Meredith said. "Lieutenant Ryder and Miss Shayne are looking into Noah's murder."

"Hell of a thing," Travers muttered. "I didn't know Kendrick all that well, but he seemed like a nice guy. Read some of the articles he wrote. The man had a real feel for the Old West, made it seem *alive* and not just a bit of dried up history."

"When was the last time you saw him?"

"Couple of weeks ago. Here at the gallery."

"You were here yesterday?"

Travers nodded. "From four-thirty to a little after seven. Todd tried calling his place a couple of times but there was no answer. By seven we figured he wasn't gonna show so we went downtown and had dinner at the Monte Carlo. Sorry I can't be of more help, Lieutenant. I heard about the killing on the radio. That's why I came by."

"Thanks for your cooperation, Mister Travers. If I have anymore questions . . . "

"You just give me a call."

Ryder smiled and turned his attention back to Todd Meredith. "Just a few more things," he said. "Background information mostly. Anything you can tell me about Kendrick's friends, personal habits, anything that will help me get a clearer picture of what he was like."

Travers reached out and touched Mattie's arm. "I'm gonna take another look at the Russells back there. Care to join me?"

She glanced at Ryder who merely shrugged. "Thanks," she said pushing her chair back. "I've been wanting to look at them up close."

They strolled slowly toward the back of the gallery, Travers curtailing his long-legged stride to Mattie's shorter steps. Walking alongside him she caught the lingering scents of tobacco and turpentine, both of them intermingled with the telltale aroma of bourbon. She decided he had the look of a man who liked his whiskey. She wondered how old he was. Somewhere between fifty and seventy, closer than that she couldn't even try to guess. The hair spilling out from beneath the brim of his hat was jet black but streaked with gray at the sides. He reminded her a little bit of an old-time western movie star, not the one who played the hero but rather the hero's friend.

They stopped far enough back so that they could take in all four canvases at once. Seeing them up close, Mattie was even more impressed. The brush strokes were broad and bold, the colors vibrant. The moving figures of cowboys, horses and steers had a raw energy that made them almost appear ready to leap out of their frames.

One painting depicted a roundup, one a lone rider on a sunset ridge. There was another of a grizzled old cowhand branding a steer and finally, her favorite, a picture of cowboys huddled around a glowing campfire at night. Each of them had Russell's stylized signature at the bottom and beneath that the little outline of a buffalo skull that was obviously his trademark.

"What do you think?" Travers asked softly.

"I think I want one, but I can't afford it."

73

He laughed. "Not unless you're rich. You could buy a good-size cattle ranch for the same price as one of those."

"I guess that lets me out."

"They're all sold, anyway. Russells never stay on the market for long. He created over four thousand works in his lifetime but there's still a tremendous demand."

Mattie nodded politely and then glanced over her shoulder. Ryder and Todd Meredith were still talking but she was too far away now to hear what was being said. Beyond them the gallery's floor-to-ceiling front window shimmered, awash with the endless spill of the rain. On the other side of the glass, cars crawled along Hennepin Avenue, bulky, slow-moving shadows in the watery half-light. A woman passed, her long legs pumping out a brisk stride, her face hidden under a tilted red umbrella. A boy in an army fatigue jacket had taken shelter in the gallery doorway. His shoulders were hunched and he kept shifting around, making short, tiny movements like some kind of experimental dance.

"You want to look at the rest of the pictures?"

She shook her head. "Not unless you've got something in the show."

"We're saving it all for my one-man. Opens November third. If you put your name and address in the guest book up front, I'll make sure you get an invitation."

"I'd like that," she said. She poked at her hair, twisting the rain-frizzled ends through her fingers. She felt suddenly uncomfortable under his silent, steady scrutiny. Not that he wasn't nice, just a little too intense. She wondered what his paintings were like. She'd have to remember to come and see his show.

She saw Ryder get up and shake hands with Meredith. She turned and smiled at Travers. "Thanks for showing me the Russells. It was nice talking with you. I'm looking foward to seeing your work."

He gravely tipped his rain-soaked Stetson. "The pleasure was all mine, pretty lady. Don't forget to sign the register by the door. I'll make sure you get that invitation."

74

On her way out Mattie dutifully printed her name and address in the open, leather-bound book. There were leaflets and catalogs stacked alongside it, one with a reproduction of Russell's sunset rider on the cover. She took one of each and stuffed them in her shoulder bag. She couldn't afford any original art on a teacher's salary—much less a Russell—but maybe Meredith would give a good price on a print or something. She turned, waved at him and then followed Ryder out into the rain.

"Did I miss anything?" she asked as they were pulling away from the curb.

"Not really," he grumbled. "Nothing we hadn't already heard. I ran Kendrick's dying words by Meredith. He brought up the cabin, too, but he didn't know what 'iron man' meant. So we're pretty much back where we started."

"Where do we go from here?"

"Over to Kendrick's print shop. I spoke to his partner, Sam Cole, this morning. He said he had to come in to do some work, so we're meeting him there."

"Fine."

"I could drop you someplace for an hour or so. I don't really need you until later this afternoon."

Mattie grinned. "That's okay," she said. "I'll just come along for the ride."

10

Kendrick & Cole Graphics was the sole occupant of a small, red-brick building on Lyndale Avenue. It had the look of a place with pretensions to be something bigger, a kind of growth-stunted, mini-Mount Vernon with too many pseudo-colonial extras tacked on for its diminutive size. Wide, slatted white shutters flanked the ground-level windows and the front entrance was dominated by a shallow portico supported by four fluted columns. Up on the roof there was a small cupola capped by a running horse weather vane, the tarnished figure shuddering drunkenly now in a gust of wind-driven rain.

Even in the unrelenting downpour the premises had a prissy, well-tended aura about them that reminded Mattie of the Kendricks' home. Without the discreet plaque beside the door, she might have mistaken the place for the offices of a prosperous law firm. Nothing about the building suggested anything as plebeian as the printing trade.

Peering through the rain-streaked windshield, Ryder followed the crescent-shaped driveway and parked the sedan alongside the portico. They got out of the car and sprinted the few feet separating them from the shelter of the portico. The glistening macadam was slippery and Mattie nearly lost her footing. She stumbled under the overhang and then winced as a blast of wind-hurled rain seeped through her collar and trickled down the back of her neck. She turned and looked at Ryder. Except for a dusting of drops across his shoulders he was untouched by the deluge.

The polished oak front door was standing slightly ajar. Ryder pushed it all the way open and ushered Mattie into a carpeted reception area with wing-back chairs and soft lighting, Japanese prints on the walls and low tables adorned with fresh-cut flowers and neatly stacked issues of *Fortune* and *Town & Country*. Understated elegance. That was the best way to describe it. It looked a little bit like Mattie's doctor's waiting room. But only if her doctor had suddenly been struck with good taste.

"Lieutenant Ryder. Please, come in."

"Mister Cole?" Ryder's tone made it a question, but one to which he already knew the answer.

"That's right" Noah Kendrick's partner said with a slow smile.

He was standing in the doorway of the inner office, a slight, white-haired man in his early sixties. As they crossed the reception area he came forward to meet them, walking very slowly. His right foot dragged along the thick carpet. His weight was partially supported by a slender, ebon-wood walking stick. Pain had cut deep lines in his narrow, ascetic face. With every step his mouth clenched hard, the thin, bloodless lips pressed tight together. His agony was so obvious that Mattie felt uncomfortable watching him. But when their eyes met, briefly, she couldn't bring herself to look away.

"Thanks for taking the time to see us," Ryder said putting out his hand. There was an awkward moment of silence while Cole shifted his walking stick to the opposite hand and stuck the right one out for Ryder to shake.

"I'm anxious to do anything I can to help," Cole said quietly. "A terrible thing. I still can't believe it. Noah gone. Murdered." His voice was still firm and clear but there was a note of bewilderment in it now, the faint tremor of loss and advancing age. He sighed and shook his head. "Everything changes," he muttered. "Why does it always seem to change for the worse?"

Ryder cleared his throat. "This is Miss Shayne," he said nodding in Mattie's direction. "She's . . . " he hesitated, "she's helping with the investigation."

78

"Nice to meet you, Miss Shayne." To Mattie's relief he made no move to shake her hand. While she murmured similar sentiments, he smiled politely, his sharp brown eyes appraising her with undisguised pleasure.

Mattie returned his unblinking stare. He was what her mother always referred to as "a *clean* old man," all pink and scrubbed looking, nattily attired in a beautifully tailored navy three-piece suit. At this distance she could smell the faint scent of his rosebud boutonniere, its fading color echoing the muted reds in his patterned silk tie. He shifted his hand on the walking stick and she noticed that the handle of it was gold and in the form of a stylized horse's head. She smiled. In another era they would have called Sam Cole a dandy. He'd probably been quite a ladies' man in his day. And from the look in his eyes, he obviously felt that that day hadn't yet passed.

They continued to stare at each other for a few more seconds, then, abruptly, he turned away. Raising his free hand, he ran his thumbnail across the neat mustache. "Shall we go into the office?" he suggested. "We can talk more comfortably there."

It turned out to be a study in contrasts. The oak paneling, deep leather chairs and dark blue carpet struck a traditional, distinctly masculine note. But it was all overlayed with softer, more feminine touches: a vase of irises on the library table, a cut-glass candy dish filled with foil-wrapped mints, two delicate-looking jade figurines. One tier of the built-in book-shelves housed a collection of antique paperweights, globes of brightly colored glass, opalescent frogs and turtles and a few multihued pieces that Mattie recognized as Millefiori. The display was certainly appropriate for someone in the printing trade but it still seemed out of place in this predominately male office. It didn't fit in with the image she'd been forming of Sam Cole.

"Most of our customers are women," Cole said, as though he'd been reading her thoughts. He paused alongside the shelf, hefted one of the weights and held it out, the pink glass glittering on his lined palm. "They are pretty," he said softly.

"Good conversation pieces too. They always seem to put the ladies at ease."

"I'm sure they do," Mattie murmured. What else could she say? She didn't care for the emphasis he'd put on *ladies*, but it was too trivial a thing to get worked up about.

She watched as Cole eased himself slowly into his desk chair. Both Mattie and Ryder were still standing. As they seated themselves, she realized that neither of them had wanted to until Cole was off his feet. That was one of the problems with a disability like that. It had a tendency to make everyone around you feel slightly guilty.

"How can I help you, Lieutenant?" Cole leaned back in his chair. His attention was totally on Ryder now.

"A little background first," Ryder said taking out his notebook. "How long have you and Kendrick been partners?"

"Thirty-one years. Thirty-one *good* years. We've both done very well, better I think than either one of us anticipated. We do several kinds of printing but our specialty is wedding invitations, stationery, things of that nature." He gestured toward the library table where a number of leather-bound sample albums were neatly laid out. "We get a lot of the society trade, if such a thing can still be said to exist." His thin lips curved into a smile that was almost self-mocking.

"You might say that I'm the front man for that. I come from one of the old, established families myself. But I turned out to be the black sheep, or at least a little gray around the edges. If America had gone in for colonies, I probably would have wound up a remittance man, sent abroad so as not to disgrace the family's good name." He turned and smiled at Mattie as though the two of them were sharing some private joke.

"Then Kendrick handled the printing end of it?" Ryder persisted.

Cole nodded. "That's right. He spent some time here at the office but his real domain was our plant in Hopkins. That's where you'll have to go if you want the smell of paper and

80

printer's ink." He sighed. "Men like Noah are rare. He was a perfectionist, a genuine craftsman."

"Now that Kendrick's dead, will his wife inherit his share of the business?"

"No, as a matter of fact she won't." The notion seemed to amuse him. "Under the terms of a long-standing agreement, I automatically inherit Noah's share as the surviving partner."

"And she's left out in the cold?"

"Hardly," Cole said with undisguised contempt. "Shortly after they were married, Noah insured his life for a quarter of a million dollars." He paused for dramatic effect and then smiled when Ryder whistled softly.

"The premiums were enormous," he continued, "but Noah wanted to make sure that Ariana was well provided for. She also gets the house, several rental properties and stock holdings. If the money is invested properly she should be comfortable for the rest of her life. Either way, I don't think she's going to have to worry about paying the light bill."

"A quarter of a million," Ryder repeated. "She didn't mention that."

"I had a feeling she might not have." Cole's thin face split in a wide grin but it never reached his hard, bright eyes.

"Do you happen to know who the carrier is?"

"Brokers Surety Life Insurance Company," Cole said without hesitation. Looking self-satisfied, he leaned forward and opened the cigarette box on his desk. The raised lid winked in the lamplight, reflecting the soft glow of inlaid wood and mother-of-pearl.

"Care for one?" he asked. As he reached inside, his gaze shifted from Mattie to Ryder.

Mattie shook her head. Ryder smiled and held up his disreputable-looking pack of Pall Malls.

Watching Cole out of the corner of her eye, Mattie sat back, enveloped by the deep leather chair. For all of Cole's manners he hadn't bothered to ask whether she minded if they smoked. Then again, this was his office and from what she'd seen so

81

far he was the kind of man who expected to have things his own way.

She watched as he lit up with a slender gold lighter. The cigarette was monogrammed, one of those extra long, Russian-style things with a cardboard mouthpiece. Give me a break, she thought. He was starting to get on her nerves, all the affectations, all the long, meaningful glances. It was kind of like being trapped in an old movie with a second-rate Charles Boyer. She sighed and took a deep breath as the air began to haze over with drifting white smoke.

"You don't like her very much?" Judging from Ryder's tone it was hardly a question.

"Ariana." Cole hunched forward, staring thoughtfully at the glowing tip of his cigarette. "I don't dislike her," he said finally. Even to Mattie's untrained ear, it sounded like a lie. "Let's just say I never completely trusted her motives. She's a very attractive young woman. Noah was considerably older, well established. Until she came along his life was his work. His experience with women of any kind was. . . . " he smiled thinly, "very limited. There's a rather crude phrase for it, but I think it applies in this case. She saw him coming."

"How would you describe their marriage?"

"Well," Cole hesitated, "I think they both got what they wanted out of it. Ariana achieved instant financial security . . . a chance to pursue her art career . . . as well as a certain standing in the deaf community." He cited the advantages in a flat, emotionless voice as though they were items on a brief but very expensive shopping list. "And Noah." Cole spread his narrow hands. "Noah got the fairy-tale princess."

Ryder looked up from his notebook. "Do you think they were happy?"

"I think they had an understanding. In this day and age it amounts to the same thing."

"*Horseshit,*" Mattie said under her breath. Sam Cole was beginning to disgust her. She shifted restlessly on the lumpy leather chair, relieved that no one had heard her whispered comment.

"Do you think she might be involved with someone else?" Ryder persisted. Mattie cut loose with a loud, long-suffering sigh but Ryder was so into this that he completely ignored her.

"An affair?" Cole looked like he was savoring the word, enjoying the taste of it in his mouth. "I don't have any proof of it, but considering the difference in their ages, I'd say it's a strong possibility."

"Any possible candidates for the lover?"

"I'm afraid not. We didn't socialize very much. Different circles, separate but not converging." He raised his index finger and made a looping motion in the air as though he were trying to inscribe some complex social galaxy with little planets that moved but never touched.

What a snob, Mattie thought. What a phony.

Ryder thumbed open a fresh page in his notebook. "Do you happen to know how the Kendricks met? Anything about her background?"

The older man winced. "As a matter of fact, I'm the one who introduced them. We use a number of calligraphers in our work, strictly on a free-lance basis. It's mostly for wedding invitations, hand-lettered names and addresses. We charge the earth but it *does* make a nice presentation."

Cole sighed and shook his head. "Ariana came in response to an ad we'd put in the paper. At the time she did calligraphy along with her painting, to help make ends meet I suppose. Anyway, her work was good and she was deaf. We always hire the hearing impaired whenever we can. So after a brief interview I sent her out to Hopkins to see Noah. The rest, as they say, is history."

Mattie smiled. From his sour expression he looked as though he wished he could rewrite it. But that wasn't going to happen. As her mother used to say, Noah Kendrick *was* history.

"What about her background?" Ryder asked.

"Strictly working class," Cole said immediately. His tone of voice made it sound more like a viral infection than a way of life.

Ryder nodded stiffly, acknowledging the information. But Mattie noticed an angry glint in his narrowed eyes, a subtle but certain hardening of his heavy features. Ryder's own roots must be blue collar as well. He was angry now but trying hard not to let it show.

Mattie watched as he reached over and ground out his half-smoked cigarette in the marble ashtray on the edge of the desk. Looking up again, he smiled tightly and said, "Could you be a little more specific, please?"

Cole looked momentarily confused, as though he knew he'd done something wrong but didn't know what it was. "Well," he said hesitantly, "both her parents are dead. At least I *think* they are. They certainly didn't show up at the wedding. Her side of the church was as barren as a toxic waste site. Just her half brother and a couple of maiden aunts."

His thin lips quirked. He seemed to be enjoying the memory. "She's a local girl," he continued. "I'm sure of that. She studied art but I can't remember where. She also went to college back east but dropped out."

"Gallaudet," Mattie said quietly. "It's in Washington, D. C. It's the oldest college for the deaf in this country, named after Thomas Hopkins Gallaudet, the man credited with bringing sign language to America. The school is a kind of Harvard for the deaf and hearing impaired. Just getting accepted there is an honor in itself."

"Is that right?" Cole commented. He sounded as though he didn't believe it.

Ryder ignored him. "What's the spelling on that?" he asked, pen poised over his notebook. When Mattie rattled it off for him, he glanced over and nodded, offering her a slight smile. Cole's class-conscious, vindictive nature seemed to be bringing them closer together.

"You knew Kendrick . . . "

A sudden blast of wind-hurled rain rattled the windowpanes, drowning out the rest of Ryder's words. Distant thunder rolled, deep-throated and ominous, like something signaling the end of the world. Cole's thin shoulders jerked violently, as if to ward off a blow from some unseen attacker. To cover his nervousness he lit another one of his ridiculous cigarettes, mouth clamped tight with concentration as he willed his fluttering hands to a rocky steadiness. He hitched his frail body around in the chair and leaned back, exhaling smoke through thin, bladed nostrils.

Mattie suddenly saw through him. Beneath that paperthin veneer, all that breeding and refinement, he was nothing more than an old man afraid of a storm.

Ryder coughed, breaking the heavy silence. "You knew Kendrick," he said, "worked with him. Can you think of anyone who might have wanted him dead?"

"Not any*one*, but two people actually." His pursed lips spread in an eery, kind of death's head smile. "The most likely candidate," he went on slowly, "is Ariana's half brother, Charlie Lentz. The man's a couple of steps above a walking vegetable, an ambulatory *crudite*. He's so spaced-out all the time that he's probably capable of anything, up to and including murder."

"You said there were two people," Ryder prodded him.

Cole nodded, holding back for a second, letting the moment build. "This other guy is also connected to Ariana, but in a different way. He's the one she dumped when she decided to go after Noah. A real hotheaded kid, militant as hell." He paused, frowning thoughtfully and then snapped his fingers. "Austin McCabe. That's his name." He thumped his desk with the head of the cane. A rose petal fell off his boutonniere and drifted down to rest on the pristine blotter.

"Did you ever hear either one of them threaten Kendrick?"

"McCabe did. I wasn't there at the time but Noah told me about it. He was very upset. It was back when Noah and Ariana first started seeing each other. Noah went by to pick her up one night and McCabe was waiting there, watching the apartment from his car. Noah and the kid got into one of those push and shove things out in the parking lot. Not a real fight, but

85

close to it. Apparently McCabe made some pretty serious threats. Stuff like Noah was going to *regret* messing with his girl . . . that he wasn't going to *live* long enough to enjoy it.''

Beaded persiration glistened on Cole's forehead. He hauled out a crisp, white handkerchief and carefully blotted it away. He seemed nervous. And it wasn't just the storm. It was almost as though in recounting the incident he felt threatened himself.

''Was there anything else? Anything more recent?''

Cole nodded, swallowing hard. ''After Noah and Ariana were married the kid would come by at night, park across from the house and just sit there for hours watching the place. When Noah would come out to confront him, he'd drive off and then come back fifteen, twenty minutes later, to start the whole thing over again. A real spooky kid.''

Ryder leaned forward. ''Did Kendrick ever report him to the police?''

''He should have,'' Cole said regretfully, ''but he didn't. Noah was too nice a guy. In this case, maybe too nice for his own good. He felt sorry for McCabe, figured he'd get over it in time. After all, he was into a pretty *heavy* thing with Ariana before Noah cut him out.'' There was an edge to Cole's voice now, a subtle emphasis on certain words that seemed to say that Ariana was responsible for all their misfortune.

''He showed up here at the office once,'' Cole continued. ''Got mad at me because I couldn't follow his signs. Kept jerking his hands around, going too fast for me. I'm a pretty fair signer. At least *Noah* always understood me. But the kid had a real attitude. As though it were my fault that I couldn't understand him.'' He sighed and looked down at his hands as if they were, in some obscure way, connected to the memory.

''He's deaf then?''

''Yes. I guess I forgot to mention that.''

''You happen to know where he lives?''

''Off of Nicollet Avenue, somewhere in the Sixties. Nicollet Village, I think the place is called.''

Frowning with concentration, Ryder hunched over his notebook taking it all down. He turned another page, leaned back and smiled. "Tell me about the half brother," he invited.

"Charlie." Cole seemed to find the very name amusing. "Charlie Lentz is one of life's losers—that's the only way to describe him. Got a million ideas, big money-making schemes, but none of the wherewithal to carry a single one of them out. He borrowed money from Noah for some kind of fast-food franchise, but that never got off the ground. Then a few weeks ago, he was back, bothering Noah for more. I don't know what the hot business prospect was this time, but Noah didn't want any part of it. He turned Charlie down flat.

"That was last week. They got into a big argument out there in the waiting room, scared the hell out of Mrs. Glen, one of my customers. Charlie was waving his arms around, shouting at Noah as if he thought he could *make* Noah hear him. Charlie isn't a very good signer. In fact he isn't much good at anything."

Cole laughed, a dry, mirthless sound coming from somewhere deep in his throat. "With Noah dead," he concluded, "Charlie can get the money from his sister to finance his half-assed schemes. I think *that's* a pretty strong motive for murder."

"It's a strong possibility," Ryder conceded. "We're certainly going to look into it."

"Damn right," Cole snapped. He looked confused, vaguely disappointed. He seemed to expect Ryder to turn handsprings in joyful abandon or, barring that, at least jump up and down in his chair. Although she didn't want to admit it, Mattie was beginning to feel sorry for the old man.

Ryder questioned him for a few more minutes, asking for Charlie Lentz's address, which Cole didn't know, and getting some more background information on Kendrick and the business. Ryder repeated the cryptic, dying message but Cole's interpretation was the same as Ariana's, that it had something to do with the fire at the cabin. Mattie tuned most of it out, sinking back in the comfortable chair, letting her mind wander while she listened to the hard, repetitious drumming of the rain.

Out in the car Mattie realized that she and Cole hadn't said good-bye, that at some point he'd dismissed her entirely, almost as though she were no longer in the room. She also realized that it didn't bother her at all, that in her own way, she'd done the same thing to him. It even gave her a kind of perverse satisfaction.

She cracked her window a half-inch as Ryder lit a fresh cigarette, spewing smoke into the confined space. The sedan's engine coughed as they crawled out of the driveway, wiper blades snickering across the streaming windshield in a rough, jerky rhythm. Beyond the hood of the car, Lyndale Avenue was all shadows and dark, flat gray, a solid sheet of rain broken in spots by the misty yellow and red blur of automobile lights. Ryder grunted, shifted the cigarette into the corner of his mouth and eased the sedan out into the traffic.

"Quite a talker," he said, eyes locked on the road. "He certainly thinks the world of Ariana Kendrick."

Mattie sighed. "He gave you a couple of good *other* suspects too. Cole should have been a marriage counselor. He's got that subtle, sympathetic touch, that uncanny ability to see a relationship from both points of view."

"All right," Ryder grumbled. "I hear you. I'm going to check out Lentz and McCabe. Hell, Cole's a suspect as well, since he inherits the business. But let's not forget that quarter of a million in insurance."

"I still don't think she killed him."

"I know," Ryder said gently. "And to a certain degree I trust your instincts. We have three more possible suspects now. But until Ariana Kendrick tells us where she was last night, she's going to be number one."

88

11

They met Sergeant Kiefer for lunch just across the city line in Richfield. The three of them took a back booth at the luncheonette in Snyder's Drug Store on Sixty-sixth. The place was quiet, the afternoon rush was already over. Scattered among the booths and along the counter, the few remaining patrons sipped coffee and read the paper or else stared out at the rain rattling against the big, plate-glass window up front.

Neither Ryder nor Kiefer mentioned the case while they ate. It was all small talk, the football scores, the rising cost of insurance and fishing licenses and, of course, this being Minnesota, the weather. When they had finished eating and the waitress had refilled their coffee cups, Ryder took out his notebook, waiting to open it until Kiefer slowly hauled out his own.

"You full too?" Sergeant Kiefer smiled at her across his half-finished bowl of chicken soup. Mattie thought he looked sick, too sick to be on duty. Patches of feverish color burned on his cheeks and his thin nose was red and tender looking. The chicken soup, with all its mythical healing powers, hadn't seemed to help any.

Unlike Ryder's leather-bound affair, the sergeant's notebook was from the dime store. The blue cardboard cover was coming loose along the top and there were tooth marks on one side of it, as though Kiefer had had to wrestle it away from the family dog.

"Let's hear it," Kiefer said picking up his pen.

Mattie sipped coffee and listened as Ryder described their meetings with Sam Cole, Meredith and Travers. She had to admit that he was good at it. His words gave shape and substance to the three men and what they'd had to say and he included small details like Cole's horsehead cane, Travers's slow, almost insolent way of talking. She could see why he made a good cop, that ability to translate observation and information into something that was vivid and real, instead of dull and plodding.

Kiefer remained quiet through the whole report, nodding to himself occasionally, his pen busily scratching away on the cheap, lined paper. But he whistled softly when Ryder told him about the quarter-of-a-million-dollar insurance policy. And when Ryder related what Cole had told him about Charlie Lentz and Austin McCabe, Kiefer's grin widened steadily. It made him look almost feline, like a scrawny old cat perched over a fish bowl.

Ryder finished, lighting another cigarette from the butt of the last. "It's getting interesting," he said. "What do you think?"

Kiefer frowned. "I think it's going in too many damned directions at once," he said morosely. "Now we've got the business partner, the half brother and the spurned lover. Not to mention the grieving widow and her friend." He shook his head. "This isn't going to play unless we can trim the cast down."

"Well, let me tell you what I got this morning," Kiefer went on. He paused and lit up another Lark, adding to the cloud of smoke that hung over the booth like a thick, indoor fog.

"There's good news and there's bad news."

Ryder groaned. "You *always* say that. You'll probably say it on Judgment Day."

Kiefer smiled. "Probably. Anyway," he said leaning back, "I got the preliminary lab report. The knife we found at the scene is definitely the murder weapon. It matches up to the stab wounds and the blood on the blade is O-negative, the same type as Kendrick's. But there weren't any prints or traces

90

of foreign substances on it, not a damn thing we could use. The lab did say, though, that the knife's new, probably never used before last night. So if worse comes to worst, we could check every retailer who carried the line.''

"That's a hell of a lot of man hours," Ryder said, shaking his head. "And it hardly ever pans out." He poked at a slab of pie with his fork, but made no move to eat it. He seemed intent on breaking the thick crust into little pieces. Maybe, Mattie thought, that's why he'd ordered it. Something to take out his frustration on.

Ryder looked on, meeting his partner's steady gaze. "Was that the good news or the bad news?" he demanded.

After a moment's consideration, the white-haired detective shrugged. "I'm not sure myself, but I've been saving the best part for last. Talking to the neighbors this morning I found out that Paul Linstrum is quite an athlete. He took part in this really grueling tricathalon thing last year. A marathon run, a hundred-mile bike race and a long-distance swim. He took second place, but the kicker is that the event's called the *Iron Man* Competion.''

"Iron man," Ryder repeated softly. "House burned down, no iron man there." He rubbed his heavy jaw and sighed. "Maybe we've got something there, but I still don't see how it connects with Kendrick's dying words. That cabin burned down last spring. So now, months later, what's so important about the 'iron man' not being there. It still doesn't make any sense."

"He said house," Mattie reminded Ryder. "Kendrick was finger-spelling the words, being very precise. If he'd wanted to sign *cabin* I'm sure that's what he would have signed."

Ryder's face tightened, the lines around his eyes standing out in sharp relief. "You're right," he said softly. "What we've got here are a bunch of leads that just don't hang together. Everything we get seems to point us in a different direction." Mattie had expected him to be angry but he just sounded tired and more than a little bit discouraged. She watched as he stubbed out his cigarette in the overflowing ashtray, grinding the butt against the ash-smeared plastic with unnecessary force. It was almost as though it were something alive, something he hated and wanted to exterminate.

"It's early days yet. We're still going to break this one wide open. Just wait and see." Even to Mattie, Kiefer's cheerful optimism sounded forced. He reached across the table and squeezed her hand. His flesh felt cold and damp, slippery with sweat. He's probably running a temperature, she thought. He should be home in bed.

"Can I borrow this lady for the afternoon?"

Kiefer's gaze shifted to Ryder who was staring down at the runny mishmash he'd made of the pie. "I want to talk to Ariana Kendrick. Try her again with the soft, subtle approach."

Ryder looked up and shook his head. "You'll have to get someone else from the department."

"All right," Kiefer said amicably. "But if that's the way you want to be, *you* can pick up the lunch check."

"Fair enough."

Mattie reached for her shoulder bag, but Ryder gently pushed her hand away. "It's on me," he insisted. "But if you're heavily into equality you can always pick up the next one."

Mattie smiled. "Fair enough, Lieutenant."

92

12

He was standing in the doorway, waiting, as though he'd somehow known ahead of time that they would be coming. A tall and lanky red-haired man in his early twenties, he watched expressionlessly as Mattie and Ryder got out of the cruiser and started up the sidewalk. He shifted his stance a little and stepped back a pace from the open doorway. His hands remained buried in the pockets of his wrinkled corduroy jacket and his gaze remained steadily on Ryder, as if he were trying to guess his weight or maybe size him up as a possible adversary.

As they narrowed the distance between them, Mattie saw that his eyes were a pale, clear blue under almost colorless lashes and that his face was dotted with freckles, like a kid who'd stayed out too long in the summer sun.

"Police," Ryder said. He pulled out his leather badge folder, flipped it open and held it out while Mattie waved her hand to get the man's attention and then made the sign for cop.

"Are you Austin McCabe?" Ryder continued. As Mattie translated the question into sign, the man's pale eyes widened and he took another step back, jerking his hands out of his pockets. His gaze shifted from Mattie to Ryder and then back to Mattie again. Finally, he nodded.

"Can we talk with you for a few minutes?"

Watching Mattie's hands, McCabe frowned and shook his head. "I'm busy," he signed. "I'm expecting someone. Maybe another time." His signs were fast and difficult to read, his freckle-dusted hands chopping at the air as though it were some invisible enemy that had to be subdued. When he made the sign for "time," tapping an imaginary wristwatch, the hard thrust of his index finger left a white impression on the skin.

Mattie voiced his reply and Ryder's face went tight with sudden anger. "Tell him this is a murder investigation," he said through clenched teeth. "He can answer some questions *here* and *now* or else we can all go down to headquarters, which will mean a lot more questions and a lot more time."

Mattie signed it just the way Ryder had laid it out. McCabe stared at them for a long moment, then shrugged and gestured for them to come in. He turned his back on them as they crossed the threshold and then led the way through a living room scattered with toys. A tow-headed boy, maybe three or four years old, was sitting in the middle of the carpet playing with a green plastic dump truck. Attached to his narrow chest by means of a harness was a small radiolike box with lines of tubing that connected it to his ears. As Mattie walked by the kid looked up. She smiled but he didn't return it.

"What the hell has that kid got on?" Ryder whispered. "Makes him look like a miniature spaceman."

"It's a body aid, a more powerful hearing aid."

Ryder frowned. "I've never seen one before. Don't deaf adults wear them?"

She looked at him and sighed. "Would *you* wear one out in the street?" she demanded. "The deaf are just as vain, just as self-conscious as the rest of us. Most of these kids don't want anything to do with a body aid by the time they hit grade school. They just want to look, well, like everyone else."

"Enlightening." Ryder nodded solemnly. "Thanks for *sharing* that with me. Isn't that what you teacher types say?"

Mattie grinned. At least he hadn't said "interesting" again.

Austin McCabe was waiting for them in the kitchen, sitting at a butcher-block table, a flower-patterned coffee mug cradled in his hands. He looked up and nodded brusquely toward the three remaining chairs. They took the two closest to McCabe.

94

As Mattie was settling in, she quickly surveyed the small kitchen. It was clean and cheerful looking, with polished brass pans hanging over the stove, crisp gingham curtains and a line of plants along the windowsill. On the counter there was a coffee maker, its glass pot nearly full. But it didn't look as though McCabe was going to offer them any. He just sat there sipping his own, maybe trying to make some kind of silent statement. He'd obviously decided that this wasn't a social occasion.

"You said something about a murder investigation," McCabe signed. "Who was murdered?"

Mattie translated and Ryder replied, "Noah Kendrick. I believe you knew him, and his wife."

Watching Mattie sign it, McCabe slowly smiled. "I read about it in the paper." In signing the last word he picked imaginary type up and set it in his palm in a motion that mimicked old-fashioned typesetting. "I'm glad he's dead," he continued. "He wasn't a nice man. But it's got nothing to do with me."

Ryder leaned back, studying him through narrowed eyes. "I'm not so sure about that," he said quietly. "You used to be involved with Ariana Kendrick. When her husband starting dating her, the two of you had a fight in the parking lot of her building. More recently, you've been harrassing the Kendricks, parking outside their place and watching it."

McCabe just stared at them for a moment, then raised his coffee mug and took a sip. "It's a free country," he signed. "I can park anywhere I want to, watch anyone I want to watch." He was signing too fast again, the words tumbling on top of one another in a blur of fluid motion. Mattie felt a headache coming on, a dull throbbing starting to build at the base of her skull. She looked away for a second, momentarily escaping the belligerent glare of McCabe's watery blue eyes.

"Where were you yesterday?" Ryder asked. "Let's say from four o'clock on?"

McCabe shrugged and dragged his open hand across his

forehead. It was the sign for "forget," the palm wiping away a memory from the mind. He put his hands back down and smiled contemptuously at Ryder, as though he were silently daring him to make a move, to play some obscure but grown-up version of push and shove.

Ryder just looked at him and sighed. "You don't remember where you were yesterday? I find that hard to believe."

"I'm not going to answer anymore questions," McCabe signed. Shifting his gaze to Ryder he slowly shook his head. "I'll talk to a deaf policeman, if you can *find* a deaf policeman. But I'm finished talking to this stupid, hearing cop." In making the "finished" sign his hands cut the air with a forceful, exaggerated finality. He looked like he was breaking something, something that only he could see.

Mattie translated it verbatim. Ryder just sat there for a few seconds, quietly staring down at his hands. Mattie expected him to be angry but when he spoke his voice was soft, surprisingly gentle. "There aren't any deaf policemen," he said. "At least not that I know of. I'm sorry you don't want to answer my questions. I'm just trying to do my job, trying to find the murderer of another deaf man. I'm not going to force the issue right now, but you're not helping yourself any by not cooperating. You think about that for a while. Because I'll be back. Maybe next time you'll have some answers for me."

Mattie saw the indecision in McCabe's face, a subtle softening of his eyes and hard-set mouth. He bit his lower lip and then raised his hands again. He looked like he was about to open up when the blond kid suddenly burst into the kitchen, hurtling himself against McCabe while one chubby hand tugged urgently at his sleeve.

The deaf man gave him a questioning stare and the boy made the sign for food and eat, tapping his mouth with his fingertips. McCabe smiled and nodded, reaching down to tousle the youngster's thick, yellow-white curls. He pushed his chair back and got a bag of cookies from the cupboard, took out two and handed them down. The boy made the sign for

96

'thank you,' then turned and raced into the living room, chunky legs pumping while a small trail of crumbs formed behind them.

"Cute kid," Mattie signed, voicing it at the same time for Ryder's benefit.

"I'm watching him for a friend," McCabe signed abruptly. He'd been close to cooperating before, but the interruption had broken the mood. Sullen animosity crowded his features again. His cold eyes shifted from Ryder to Mattie as though he were trying to figure out why they were still there.

"I'm expecting company," he signed. "I have things to do now. We've talked long enough."

When Mattie voiced it, Ryder nodded resignedly and shoved back his chair. The three of them rose from the table together, McCabe eyeing Ryder warily as though he suspected the big cop might try and boost the rest of the cookies. Mattie wondered if McCabe had had trouble with the police before. He seemed like a man who didn't deal well with authority. She imagined that Ryder had already made a mental note to check if he had any criminal record.

Mattie trailed Ryder into the toy-strewn living room and then stopped and turned at the touch of McCabe's hand on her arm. "I'm not really glad Kendrick's dead," he signed urgently. "I hated him when he took Ariana away from me, but I didn't kill him." His freckled face had gone passive, almost slack, and he looked as though he were more than a little bit embarrassed.

"Anyway, it's all over between Ariana and me. I'm seeing somebody else now." He gestured down at the boy who was hunched over the toy dump truck again, tossing bits of cookie into the back. "It's his mother. We've been going out for a couple of weeks now. I haven't been anywhere near the Kendricks since then."

Mattie nodded. "What about yesterday?" she signed. "Why don't you tell me where you were? It would make it easier for all of us."

McCabe spread his hands. "Right here," he signed. "Alone, all day. No way to prove it." He smiled crookedly. "But it happens to be the truth."

As Mattie nodded again, he turned toward the coffee table and picked up a slender stack of snapshots. He sighed, shook his head and handed them to her.

"I got these out this morning," he signed, "when I read about Kendrick's death in the paper." Mattie peered down at the top photo. It showed McCabe and Ariana Kendrick standing in front of a ski lodge, their faces brightly lit by the sun reflecting off the snow. They looked cold but happy, their bodies bundled up in down vests and mufflers, their arms wrapped around each other as they faced the camera. It was a picture of two people very much in love. Mattie knew it instinctively; she could almost feel the lens-captured power of it, love relentless, unquestioning and naive. She took a deep, slow breath and shuffled through the rest of the stack. The remainder were mostly of Ariana alone, sitting by a fireplace, building a snowman, standing awkwardly at the crest of a ski slope. She looked happy, somehow younger in all of them. Like someone else in another life.

Mattie handed them back to McCabe but didn't keep her hands up to sign. It was one of those moments. There wasn't anything to say.

Grinning at her, McCabe gripped the corners of the stack and slowly and purposefully ripped the snapshots in two. Mattie's mouth dropped open but she still didn't sign anything. She watched as he held the pieces in his hand and carried them over to the open window by the door. The rain had stopped a half hour earlier but the sky was still a dark, brooding smoke gray. In a single easy motion he scattered them to the wind. The photo fragments twisted and spun for a moment, riding the current of air before the wind slapped them back against the front of the house. "It's over," signed McCabe. "It's got nothing to do with me anymore." He rubbed his palms across each other in a gesture of brushing away something that had been stuck there too long.

98

Mattie nodded, smiled to show she understood. Leaning against the wall by the door, Ryder loudly cleared his throat. She glanced at him and then back at McCabe. The deaf man smiled and put out his hand. After a moment's hesitation, Mattie shook it. Heading for the door, she looked back one last time and the little blond boy waved at her shyly, his pudgy fingers gently stroking the air.

"What happened to the *interpreting*?" Ryder demanded out on the sidewalk. "I saw a lot of signing but I didn't hear anything." He stopped abruptly and took out his cigarettes, cupping his hands around the match to shield it from the wind.

"It wouldn't have worked," Mattie said softly. "He would have seen me voicing it and that would have been the end. Maybe he was just more comfortable with me; I understand sign and I'm not exactly what you'd call intimidating. Anyway, it was all pretty personal stuff." She went on to relate what he'd told her, her impressions of the photographs and Mc-Cabe's unverifiable alibi for the time of the murder.

Ryder took a deep drag on the cigarette and slowly exhaled smoke. "Strange kid," he muttered. "Lots of anger there, but underneath it he's probably not a bad guy. It can't be easy being deaf. I guess he's one of those militant types you were telling me about."

"I guess so," Mattie said smiling. Her gaze drifted back to the front of the house, focusing on the border of crushed stone and shrubs where the torn picture pieces had finally landed. Impulsively she strode back up the walk, knelt down and began to collect them. Ryder ambled up and peered over her shoulder.

"What are you doing?"

"I'm not sure," she admitted, "but I hate to see them just lying there. Maybe he'll change his mind and want them back. Maybe he won't. But I don't feel right about leaving them. It's funny how yesterday's dreams turn into today's litter." She edged the fragments into a neat pile, slipped them in her shoulder bag, stood up and brushed off her hands.

"I think you're a sentimentalist."

Mattie sighed. "Probably."

"If it's any consolation, I don't think he did it. The timing is all wrong for one thing. If McCabe had wanted to murder Kendrick he would have done it long ago, not months after they were married. And that parking in front of the house is just kid's stuff, a way of letting off some steam."

Mattie looked up and grinned at him. "Well, I can't believe you actually think someone is *innocent*. It makes for a nice change. Maybe there's hope for you yet."

"I don't think he's a *likely* suspect," Ryder said frowning. "But he isn't completely out of the running yet. Especially with that uncheckable alibi." He reached out and touched Mattie's arm, his fingertips just brushing the fabric of her coat. They turned and began to walk back to the car.

"You know what his real problem is?"

Mattie shook her head.

"He's still in love with her."

13

Charlie Lentz's address turned out to be an apartment building, downtown on the fringes of Loring Park. The place had somehow missed the ongoing renovation of the past ten years; standing between two spruced-up, freshly painted stuctures, it looked untouched by anything except time.

It was one of those geographically misplaced but popular twenties Spanish deals, with an arched front door flanked by spiraled pillars and a stucco facade with little wrought-iron balconies under the windows. But the stucco was grimy and chipped, stained the reddish-brown of dried blood in spots where rusty runoff had seeped down from the balconies. On the dirt-streaked fanlight above the door, the name CASA LOMA GARDENS was spelled out in flaking gilt letters. From the look of the place any gardens it might have had were too far gone even to be a memory.

Mattie followed Ryder up the narrow sidewalk. The concrete was cracked and uneven, with clusters of tall, autumn-yellowed grass sprouting up through the fissures like tufts on an old man's beard. Mattie shivered, bunching the fabric of her trench coat pockets around her cold fingers. The rain had stopped while they were inside the restaurant but it looked like it might start up again any minute. The sky was a deep slate gray, low and brooding. The hovering storm clouds had a hard, decisive quality as though they'd been painted into the wet sky with brush strokes of dark color.

In the small, dimly lit vestibule, Ryder scanned the bank of brass mailboxes. The last one on the left had Lentz's name on it, along with the number six. Ryder moved to press the bell beneath it and then stopped short, pulling his hand back. He turned and tried the inner door. It wasn't locked.

"You're not going to ring first? See if he's home?" Mattie asked.

Ryder glanced at her with a tight smile. "Let's just say I like surprises. Besides, in a dump like this the doorbells probably don't work anyway."

He shouldered open the door and then held it for Mattie. Units one and two were on the ground floor, so Lentz was at the top of the three-story building. Trailing Ryder again, Mattie mounted the stairs, her damp soles squeaking on the worn rubber runner. The inside of the place was surprisingly clean. The hallway reeked of disinfectent and in the murky light she could see that the balusters and baseboards had recently been cleaned and polished.

On the second-floor landing, spicy cooking smells intermingled with the eye-watering odor of ammonia and from behind one of the apartment doors Mattie heard snatches of soft, high-pitched conversation. It sounded like Vietnamese, but she couldn't be sure. There were a lot of Southeast Asian refugees in the Twin Cities. They were ambitious, hard-working people for the most part. Also very clean. Their presence in the building just might account for the spotless condition of the halls.

By the time they reached the third floor Ryder was short of breath, rasping and huffing like an old locomotive on a steep grade. He tried to cover it up with a fake coughing spell, but he didn't fool Mattie. And he certainly wasn't fooling himself. If he couldn't quit smoking he should at least try and cut down, she thought. She was about to say something to that effect when he reached out suddenly and shoved her back against the wall.

"Hey," she protested. "You don't . . . "

He held up his hand, signaling silence, then nodded toward the apartment door. "Lock's been jimmied," he whispered. "Scratch marks are still fresh." He eased his service revolver clear of the holster and drew a deep, ragged breath. "Stay clear of the doorway," he cautioned her. "Don't try to come in until I tell you it's safe. There might still be someone in there."

She nodded wordlessly but he didn't see her. He was already in motion, shouting "police" as he kicked open the door and moved quickly through it in a low crouch.

Mattie could hear her own hammering heartbeat. Her mouth tasted dry and her hands were shaking. Pressing tight against the wall, she listened to Ryder's muffled footsteps, a soft, echoing tread from somewhere inside. What if she heard gunshots? She suddenly realized that they hadn't talked about *that*. Would she try to help him? But how? Or would she run like hell at the first loud noise?

Three long minutes later he poked his head back out, a sudden, jack-in-the-box movement that startled Mattie. "Come on in," he said grinning. "There's nobody home." He shoved the door back for her. His gun was now nowhere in sight. She started in and then hesitated on the threshold. "Should we be in there if Lentz isn't home? I mean . . . it just doesn't seem right."

Ryder turned and sighed. "The lock was broken," he said patiently. "I have reason to suspect forced entry, a possible burglary in progress. That's reason enough for me to check out the scene. You *want* to wait in the hall?" he said shrugging. "That's fine with me. I'll even give you the keys to the car if you think you'll be more comfortable there." Without waiting for her reply, he turned on his heel and stalked inside, letting the door swing shut behind him.

"It was just a question," Mattie muttered to herself. She shoved the door open with unnecessary force and stomped into the apartment.

"Keep your hands in your pockets," Ryder called out from somewhere in the rear. "I don't want you touching anything."

"I don't think I *want* to touch anything," she said.

The small living room where she was standing had long ago

surrendered to dust and general neglect. Maybe Charlie Lentz cared about something, but the place where he lived wasn't it.

The scant furnishings had been old and shabby to begin with, a ratty-looking studio couch, two scratched end tables, some thrift store bookcases and a coffee table and two fifties motel-room lamps, their lopsided drum shades age-stained a yellowy, nicotine brown. A thick, gritty layer of dust coated all the flat surfaces and particles of it swirled lazily, moving in slow motion as they rode the currents of stale air. There were a few signs of life, or at least recent occupancy. A succession of beer bottles had cut fresh circles in the end table dust; four of the Grain Belt empties were clustered on the coffee table, one with a half-inch of flat beer still inside. The television set was on, a rolling black-and-white picture without any sound.

Mattie watched the old western movie it was tuned to for a couple of seconds, but the barrel-roll reception was an invitation to a headache that she didn't need. Shifting her gaze from the screen, she looked up at the heavy brass light fixture overhead. It was threaded with cobwebs and filmed with dust. There were more burned-out bulbs than live ones. Still it was a nice Deco period piece. That probably meant it belonged to the building and not Lentz.

She wandered over to the bookcases to inspect their contents. Ariana's half brother was strictly a paperback man, all nonfiction and from the look of it, all secondhand. The titles were mostly self-help and get-rich-quick, things like *Harness Your Psychic Money-Making Powers*, *The Thirty-Day Wealth Plan* and *Dream Yourself Rich!* Sighing, Mattie looked away. Whatever promises the paperbacks had made, the systems and formulas obviously hadn't worked for Charlie Lentz. Maybe he'd never even tried them, at least not all the way through.

She was beginning to get a picture of him, one of life's habitual losers, a man of half-done, halfhearted schemes and dreams. The aura of his cumulative failure seemed to hang over the apartment, clinging to everything, as thick, gray and all-prevailing as the dust.

Feeling almost sorry for him, Mattie meandered into the dining alcove and then stopped abruptly, a few feet shy of the rickety-looking card table. Along with a pair of matching chairs, it was the only furniture in the narrow room. But what had pulled her up short was the partially eaten slice of pizza on the table. Mold had started to form along the edges and the odor it gave off was definitely not Italian. Mattie took a quick, shallow breath, turned and walked back to the living room. She decided to pass on the rest of the tour. Especially the kitchen. There were probably new life forms in the refrigerator, stuff that bacteriologists hadn't even dreamed about.

"Isn't this guy something?" Ryder said cheerfully. He sauntered into the living room holding a wrinkled ticket folder, his heavy fingers gripping it along the edge as though he were afraid of damaging it. "I've seen some dumps in my day," he continued, "but this place is truly gross. Lentz must have gotten his interior decorator from the back pages of *Soldier of Fortune* magazine."

"What have you got there?" Mattie nodded toward the paper folder he was holding.

"It's a used Trailways bus ticket. Round-trip. You'll never guess where?"

"You're right," Mattie said agreeably. "I'm not going to guess. Why don't you just tell me?"

"Lake Vermillion." He was grinning now and he stretched the name out as he said it, his voice deep and resonant as a game show announcer's. "It's from last spring," he went on. "April eleventh departure from the Cities, the thirteenth on the return. Not a very long vacation, but long enough for a little bit of arson."

"Is that when the Kendricks' cabin burned down?"

"I think so." Ryder bit his lower lip, lost in thought for a few seconds. "I'm almost positive," he said finally, "but I have to check the dates to make sure."

Mattie studied him silently for a moment. His enthusiasm was almost contagious. He was like a little kid with a new, unexpected toy. She was glad to see him pulling out, even momentarily, from his earlier depression. He wasn't the easiest man in the world to like, but then there were his partner's suicide and the work itself. It would take a heavy toll on anyone. But especially on someone like Ryder. Someone who cared.

"You can tie him in with the arson then?" It was an obvious question, but she asked it anyway. He seemed anxious to talk, to draw out the high.

"If I'm right," he said nodding, "I can put him near the scene. But torching the cabin's only secondary. If he hated Kendrick enough to do that, it's possible that he hated him enough to take his life." Ryder dug out his cigarettes and lit up one, hungrily drawing in the smoke. His eyes didn't look so tired anymore; the bluish-gray irises gleamed with an almost feverish excitement.

He smiled at Mattie and said, "Now all we have to do is find the guy. Bring him in for questioning. I'll put out a description and a man in an unmarked car to watch the building."

"You really think he's the one?" she asked softly. "Somehow it seems like," she hesitated, slowly surveying the sad, dingy room. "It seems as though he wouldn't have it *in* him, have the guts for something as big as murder." She kept her voice neutral, almost cautious. She had some doubts but she didn't want to rain on Ryder's parade.

He looked away from her, down at the glowing tip of his cigarette. "I don't *know* anything for sure," he said quietly. "But this could be a solid lead, a direction to go in. At the moment Lentz is a loose end, a possible arsonist who might have moved up to murder. As for him not having the 'guts,' I once brought in this mild-mannered, sad sack of a guy who wacked out his entire family with a fire ax."

Mattie nodded, swallowing hard. "You talked about putting out a description of him. You know what he looks like?"

"I found his passport in the bedroom. Never been used. There's a family picture over here if you're curious." She followed Ryder past the couch to the farthest end table. The framed picture had fallen flat and was partially hidden by the base of the lamp. A fine layer of dust coated the glass but the image was still clear enough. "That's our boy," Ryder said solemnly.

The photograph could have been titled "Beauty and the Beast." Mattie recognized Ariana Kendrick immediately. Her hair was longer and windblown, her face a little less sharp, still holding the softness of late childhood. But it was unmistakably Ariana. The man beside her was fat and round-shouldered, with a pudgy, petulant face, sallow skin and greasy-looking, slicked-back black hair. He was peering suspiciously at the photographer, his dark eyes blurred by thick, black-rimmed glasses. Something in his expression seemed to say that this wasn't one of those moments he wanted recorded for posterity.

Mattie almost missed the background, seeing it but not really *seeing* it. But something familiar pulled her back, the shape of the building, the curving line of trees. It was the refreshment pavillion by Lake Calhoun. This long-ago picture had been taken just a stone's throw away from where Noah Kendrick had been left to die.

14

After a quiet dinner alone, Mattie washed the dishes, poured herself the last of the coffee and carried it into the living room. Her footsteps echoed loudly on the polished wood floor and from outside she could hear the small night sounds, little creaks and groans and whispers, barely audible under the steady droning of the wind. The house usually seemed warm and cheerful, a safe, solid place of refuge. But tonight there was a curious emptiness to it all, something she felt but really couldn't define. Maybe it was just the long, busy day with Ryder. Or maybe it wasn't anything at all. *Whatever* it was, she was probably better off not thinking about it.

She settled into the platform rocker with her coffee and a paperback book. But after a couple of pages she gave up trying to read. Putting down the book she leaned back and closed her eyes. She wondered what Ryder was up to now. Probably still working. In spite of everything, she had to admit that she liked him. Not that there was anything to it, no possibility of a relationship. But he was an interesting man. Complex, often angry, frequently frustrating, but *definitely* interesting.

Mattie sighed and took a sip of her coffee. Part of Ryder's charm, if you could call it that, was what he did for a living. Although she'd never dream of telling him, she'd always been fascinated by police work, by detection and mysteries, problem solving of any kind. She'd also been a real mystery story junkie as a kid. In the attic of her grandmother's house in Mankato there were still dusty stacks of Cherry Ames and Trixie Belden books, the stuff of a thousand long-ago rainy summer days. She was grown up now, although she sometimes hated to admit it, but she still loved a good mystery.

Only Noah Kendrick's murder wasn't something out of a book. She'd seen him dying, stood in touching distance of death in all its cold, grim finality. It made her angry and it made her want to help find whoever it was that did it. There were too many suspects and motives, and hardly any alibis at all. She knew Ryder still thought that Ariana Kendrick was the prime contender. The woman had lied about her whereabouts last night. There was also the fact that her husband's death made her a wealthy woman, independent and secure, free to marry again, someone nearer her age this time, devote herself to her art, whatever she wanted to do. Was Paul Linstrum a part of her plans for the future? On the surface it didn't look that way but the two of them were trying to cover up something. Otherwise why had they lied about being in Ariana's studio all evening?

Then there was Ariana's half brother. Although she hadn't met Charlie Lentz yet, Mattie had a strong sense of him from his shabby apartment and the run-ins with Kendrick that Sam Cole had described. An angry loser, fueled by his own frustration, would he commit murder in the hope of easy access to Ariana's new-found fortune? Cole was a possibility, but not a very strong one. He had Kendrick's share of the business now, but he seemed to be wealthy in his own right. As for Austin McCabe, Mattie agreed with Ryder. The timing was all wrong. But he still didn't have an alibi for the evening of the murder.

Todd Meredith and Neil Travers didn't seem to figure into it at all. And then at the center of everything was Kendrick's strange, dying message: *House burned down . . . no iron man there.* It vaguely fit several elements of the case, the fire at the cabin, Linstrum winning second place in the Iron Man Competition. But as Ryder kept on reminding her, it just didn't make any sense.

Mattie swallowed some more coffee, but it was cold and brackish-tasting now, not worth the bother of heating up. She put the cup down by her chair, stood up, stretched, and rubbed

110

her arms. It was chilly enough tonight for a fire. It would cheer her up a bit too, which was something she definitely needed. She started toward the back of the house where the firewood was stacked outside the kitchen door. But the sudden, shrill ringing of the telephone checked her stride. Muttering under her breath, she spun around and hurried to answer it.

"Hello," Mattie panted into the receiver.

"Hello, yourself." It was Peter, calling long distance from New York. In spite of the miles, the connection was crystal clear, the familiar voice deep and resonant, as confident as ever.

"How are you?" she asked. It was a stupid question because Peter was always *fine*. But she asked it anyway. It was a way of filling up the quiet, a part of their telephone ritual.

"I'm fine," he assured her. "Never better. Business is good, maybe too good. I barely have any time for myself anymore. But I can't complain. How about you?"

"I'm fine. Still getting settled in, getting used to working again. But everything's okay."

"You sound a little tired."

"I had a busy day."

"On Saturday?" He sounded incredulous. "You're not working a weekend job or anything, are you? Because if it's a question of money I can . . . "

"It's nothing like that," Mattie interrupted him. "Just a bunch of errands I had to run." She wasn't sure why she lied, but just that she didn't want to tell him about Ryder and the murder investigation. They were a part of her new life and Peter and New York were a part of the old. What separated them was a flimsy barrier made of distance and time, a shaky wall in need of constant reinforcement.

"I was thinking of flying out next month."

Mattie took a deep, slow breath and sat down on the stairs, the receiver cradled between her head and shoulder. "Peter," she said softly, "I don't think that would be a very good idea."

There was a long silence on the other end of the line. Finally he cleared his throat and said, "Sid Heilberg called you the other day and left a message on your machine. I still think you should accept some sort of settlement. It doesn't have to . . . "

"No," Mattie cut in. "We've been over all this before. There's nothing more to talk about." She tried to keep the exasperation out of her voice, but she could hear it herself, a hard, knife-edge shrillness that made her sound old and bitter.

Peter sighed. "All right. But feel free to change your mind."

She was about to tell him that she had no intention of doing so when the doorbell rang, the noisy trill of it suddenly filling the empty house. "Damn," Mattie muttered looking at the front door and then back at the phone. "I've got to go," she said quickly. "There's someone at the door."

"I love you." Peter's voice was low, barely above a whisper.

"Take care of yourself," she said gently. "'Bye."

She cradled the receiver and pushed herself off the stairs as the bell rang again. "All right already," she muttered as she wrapped her hands around the knob and yanked open the heavy door. She didn't know whom or what to expect, but she had to admit she was pleasantly surprised. Standing on her front porch was Lieutenant Ryder and a large bottle of wine.

"I'm not interrupting?" he asked sheepishly. He seemed suddenly interested in his shoes, peering down at them while his big hands shifted the wine bottle around as though it was something that had gotten too hot to hold.

"No, you're not interrupting. I was just on the phone. Come on in." She stepped back as he crossed the threshold and Mattie shoved the door closed behind him, hurriedly shutting out the chill night air. As she turned from the door, Ryder pressed the bottle into her hands. Mattie smiled. It was almost as if he were afraid someone would see him with it. She got the feeling that he didn't do this very often, that bringing wine to a woman was something new, like a trip to a foreign country where you knew the language in theory but not in practice.

"I thought you might like that," he said solemnly.

112

"Looks nice. Thank you very much." The dark green glass was cold and slightly slippery to the touch. The label proclaimed it to be something French but nothing that Mattie had ever heard of before. A corner of a bright orange sticker still adhered to the bottle. That meant the offering was from the bargain bin, the land of Chateau Schwartz. But, she quickly reminded herself, it really was the thought that counted.

"Let me get a couple of glasses and open this up." Ryder followed in her wake as he headed back toward the kitchen. "I was thinking about building a fire," she continued. "It's a good night for it."

"Great idea."

"If you want to help, the wood's out by the back steps."

"I'll get it then," he said nodding. He sounded eager, seemed almost relieved to have something to do. He disappeared out the back door and came back a minute later, his arms piled high with a heavy pyramid of logs. Grunting softly, he lumbered out of sight again leaving a tiny trail of bark and wood chips on the kitchen floor.

Listening to his footsteps echo through the house, Mattie grinned and gave the corkscrew another twist. Watching Ryder reminded her of something her mother used to say, that it was nice to have a man around the house, if only to do the heavy lifting.

She poured the wine, put some cheese and crackers on a tray along with it and carried it into the living room. Ryder already had the fire going but he remained hunkered down in front of the hearth, eyeing it critically. Mattie set the tray down and walked over to stand beside him.

"Nice," she murmured putting her hands out. The warm, steady updraft felt good against her skin, almost like a forgotten sensation, a pleasant moment only vaguely remembered from childhood. Ryder smiled up at her, his face bathed in the bright, reflected colors of the flames. "I think that about does it," he said rising. He brushed the last of the wood chips from his hands, took a glass of wine and settled into the platform rocker.

Mattie moved one of the rattan chairs alongside, curled her legs up and took a small, exploratory sip of the wine. It was surprisingly good—dry with a nice bouquet. She smiled at Ryder across the rim of her glass. "Is this a social visit, Lieutenant?"

"About half-half."

"I'm glad you came over."

Ryder smiled, seeming to relax a little more. He sipped his wine and shifted around, settling more comfortably into the rocker. "There's also been some developments in the case," he said. "I did a little checking on Kendrick's partner, Sam Cole. It turns out he's a heavy gambler, *very* heavy in fact. He's got markers out all over town. I found out that he owes one bookie forty grand. He also has a taste for the ladies, the young expensive kind. And that bum leg of his isn't an old war wound or anything like that. It's a souvenir from a couple of hard cases who got overly enthusiastic in collecting an overdue debt."

"Loan sharks?"

Ryder nodded, placed the wedge of cheese on a cracker and took a bite. A few stray cracker crumbs dropped down to cling to the hairy tweed of his jacket. Mattie resisted a strong impulse to lean over and brush them off.

"You said developments?" she prompted.

Ryder swallowed and took a sip of wine. "It probably doesn't mean anything," he said dismissively. "But Kiefer went through Kendrick's papers at the house and came across an article he'd been working on for one of those western magazines. It was all about prairie fires and a big section of it dealt with a ranch that got burned out."

"A ranch *house*."

"Yeah, that was part of it."

"Maybe that's it then, what Kendrick's dying message was all about?"

"I don't think so," Ryder said shaking his head. "The fire was in nineteen-ten. A *bit* too early, I'd say, to tie in with all

114

this." He shrugged and smiled at her. "Still, it is an interesting coincidence and I thought you might like to hear about it."

"Thanks. I appreciate you telling me everything." She hesitated, then smiled. "Earlier today, I wasn't so sure you'd keep your end of the deal."

"I try to keep my promises."

The conversation seemed to die at that point, both of them aware of the gradually deepening silence. Mattie poured more wine and cut herself a hunk of cheese and ate it slowly, as though the drawn-out activity would somehow offset the quiet. Ryder took out his cigarettes, lit one and smoked it while he stared at the fire. In the shifting firelight his bearded face looked thoughtful and brooding, like a man confronting old, unwelcome memories.

Finally he cleared his throat and turned to look at Mattie again. "You're a teacher, right? You work with deaf kids?" There was a touch of the interrogator in his tone. After all those years as a policeman he probably wasn't even aware of it. It didn't bother Mattie. At least he sounded as though he were interested in what she had to say.

"I'm an itinerant teacher for District two-eighty-seven," she explained. "It kind of makes me sound like a gypsy, which is partly true. What I do is travel to several different schools each day and work with deaf and hearing-impaired students who are mainstreamed there."

"Mainstreamed?"

"Sorry," she muttered. "I have a tendency to lapse into *educationalese*. It's one of the hazards of the profession. Mainstreaming is when students with special needs are placed in a regular school environment. We offer them support, interpreting, counseling, anything that will help them to fit in."

"It must be hard. For the kids I mean?"

Mattie nodded. "It isn't easy living with a hearing loss. The sense of separation, of alienation, can sometimes be overwhelming. After the Second World War the group of veterans with the highest suicide rate were artillery men who suffered a hearing loss while working around the big guns. Another thing about deafness is that it's almost an *invisible* disability. If someone is blind you see the guide dog, the white cane; a paraplegic or a quad is usually identifiable by the wheelchair. But when you see someone with a hearing loss, they *look* like everyone else. And somehow that just makes it harder. There's that sense of normalcy without it really being that way."

She sighed and shook her head. "My kids do pretty well, though. Most of them work hard and play hard too. They want to get everything they can out of life."

Ryder regarded her thoughtfully. "You like teaching a lot, don't you?"

"I love it," Mattie admitted. "And finally, after a lot of years, teaching is *starting* to get the recognition it deserves. It used to be when you told someone you were a teacher the only reaction you'd get was a kind of enormous cosmic yawn. People saw it as a second-class profession, something you did because you weren't good enough to compete in the 'real' world. But that's beginning to change now. Maybe it has something to do with the fact that all the baby boomers are grown up now and starting to have kids of their own. Suddenly teaching is creative and challenging. Of course, it's always been that way. People just didn't see it before."

"I know what you mean," Ryder said nodding. "There's a big difference between what police work *is* and what people perceive it to be. But enough of that. Tell me more about yourself. What made you choose deafness as a field to specialize in?"

Mattie hesitated for a moment, taking a sip of wine and then carefully setting her glass on the table. "It's a family thing," she said quietly. "Back when I was just starting college, my older sister, Sarah, and her husband had their first child. A little girl they named Ashley. As she got older they realized she wasn't responding to certain stimuli. The first doctor they took her to diagnosed her as retarded. But then they took her to a specialist and after a lot of testing it turned out she had

116

a severe hearing loss. It was a very difficult time, especially for Sarah. Being off at school there wasn't much I could do to help. But I started researching the field, to send them the latest information, and I got so interested it turned into my major. You should see Ashley now,'' she said grinning. "She's fourteen, devastatingly pretty and incredibly bright.''

"I'd like to meet her sometime.''

"Maybe you will.''

Ryder lit another cigarette and leaned back in the chair. "You've always been a teacher then?''

"Except for this past year.'' She paused for a second, eyeing him over the rim of her glass. Why not, she thought? It was probably time she started talking about it instead of keeping it all inside. "I took some time off to get married. Only it didn't work out.''

"Oh.'' The exclamation was followed by an awkward moment of silence. Except for the crackle of the fire the stillness in the room was absolute. Then Ryder abruptly raised his glass, drained it and set it on the table next to Mattie's. "Tell me about it,'' he said, looking at her directly. "If you want to talk, I'm a good listener. Hell, that's mostly what police work is all about. And I really want to know, not because I'm curious, but because I like you and this was obviously something important in your life.'' He sighed audibly and took a drag off his cigarette. "There are moments,'' he said exhaling smoke, "when I wish I were better at saying things.''

She leaned over and touched his hand. "I know what you're saying,'' she assured him. "And I appreciate it. As for the marriage, there's not a whole lot to tell.'' She got up and crossed to the fire, suddenly feeling the need for a little distance between them.

"In a way it's funny that I should be telling you about Peter, because that's who I was talking to on the phone when you arrived. He lives in New York. That's where we met and where I lived when we were married.''

"You like it out there?''

"I thought so at the time."

"What was he like?"

Mattie considered the question for a moment, trying to be fair. "He's extremely handsome, well-mannered and well-to-do. He comes from one of those old eastern society families with so much money it makes your teeth hurt. Peter works very hard, though. He's a partner in a brokerage firm on Wall Street. High-pressure stuff but vaguely glamorous in a pinstripe kind of way." Smiling crookedly she picked up the poker and began to jab at the crumbling log. Little showers of sparks flew up like miniature fireworks from some long-postponed Fourth of July.

"When we first met," she said softly, "I thought he had a lot of depth and character. But the character turned out to be good manners, surface charm and all that depth turned out to be the shallow end of the pool."

"So you left him?"

"No. At least not until I came home early from some classes I was taking and found him in bed, our bed, with this bimbo from his office. *Then* I left him. Ten minutes to pack a bag, then fifty-three minutes later I was on the next flight out of LaGuardia."

"You don't mess around." There was something close to awe in his voice.

"No, I don't," she said emphatically. "And I didn't expect him to either." She poked at the log with renewed vigor, setting off another explosion of bright sparks.

"So now you're divorced, a part of America's fastest-growing majority."

"Almost. It won't be final until next month. Peter and his lawyer keep trying to get me to accept some kind of settlement. I suppose it's conscience money on Peter's part. If he can get me to take a big hunk of it, he won't feel so bad."

"But you don't want anything?" The way Ryder said it, it wasn't even a question.

"Not a dime."

118

"Why not?"

Mattie shrugged. "We were only married nine months. So it's not as though there was any community property to split up. And I'm perfectly capable of supporting myself." She turned away from the fire and looked at Ryder, a slow smile gradually edging up the corners of her mouth. "Besides that and maybe most important of all, I don't *want* Peter to feel any better."

15

Later that night Mattie had the dream again.

It carried her back to the graveyard with its patchwork shadows, crooked tombstones and the bright moon overhead that lit the scene like some macabre stage set. She was kneeling just as before. A cold, sharp wind whipped her hair around. Her legs felt cramped, the muscles knotted up with pain. She knew, but not how or why, that she *couldn't* move. Something was keeping her here, willing her to stay.

In horror and fascination she stared down at the black, fresh-turned earth and the multitude of scarred and twisted hands that sprang from it. They never stopped moving; the long, blood-caked fingers twitched and jerked in a senseless, obscene parody of sign. She wanted to look away but couldn't. She raised her own hands, then suddenly froze, feeling the presence behind her. She snapped her head around and . . .

Mattie sat up suddenly, kicking off the bedclothes. She was breathing hard and fast and the ragged pounding of her heart seemed incredibly loud in the hushed night quiet of the bedroom. She blinked her eyes and took a deep, calming breath. It had been the dream again. The same damned dream as before.

Shivering, she hitched the comforter up to cover her bare shoulders and peered at the clock on the bedside table. According to the hands on the luminous dial it was a few minutes past two in the morning. Mattie groaned, sank back on the pillow and squeezed her eyes shut. The best thing to do was to go right back to sleep, but that was easier said than done.

Her head was buzzing from the wine. Her mouth felt dry

and her tongue seemed to be coated with a tart, metallic aftertaste, a reminder of the vino's dubious vintage. Not that she was complaining. She'd had a wonderful time. And because tomorrow was Sunday she could sleep it off. But what she needed right now was a couple of aspirin and as much water as she could gulp down.

She sat up again, pushed the covers back and swung her legs over the side of the bed. The wooden floor was cold and after a couple of misses, she managed to thrust her feet in her fleece-lined moccasins. She grabbed her robe off the chair, slipped it on and cinched it at the waist. Still half-asleep, she padded toward the bathroom and then suddenly froze.

The noise was soft but distinctive. Footsteps, coming from somewhere down in the living room. Outside the wind had died down and except for the random night murmuring of the house, the silence was deep and unbroken. For a few seconds she was ready to believe that it was just her imagination. But then they started up again, a little louder than before. Footsteps, definitely footsteps.

Mattie swallowed hard. Turning slowly, she eased open the drawer of the nightstand. The .45 Army automatic was there in its accustomed place, wrapped in a soft chamois pouch and smelling faintly of gun oil. She carefully slipped it out of the drawstring bag, snicked off the safety and then, using a two-handed grip, leveled at the dark, open door of the bedroom.

It felt good in her hands, solid and comforting, almost as though Uncle Red were there with her, sweat dripping off his broad forehead, the beer bottles shattering, filling the hot, dusty air with bright, whirling shards of glass. Mattie slowly lowered the gun, took a deep breath and walked softly toward the door.

The house was quiet again. Maybe whoever it was had already gone. Then she heard it, the same muffled footfalls, only fainter now, as though the intruder had worked his way to the back of the house, either the dining room or the kitchen.

Knowing she was now wasting valuable time, she forced

122

herself to move forward into the darkness of the hallway. She tried to walk as softly as possible but her leather-soled moccasins brushed the bare floor with a telltale whispery swishing sound and every few feet, the cold floorboards creaked and groaned like an old man moving restlessly in a dream-troubled sleep. She stopped at the end of the hall and peered cautiously down the shadowed staircase.

Pale light from a street lamp seeped through the glass in the upper half of the front door. The shadows in the hall below were long and deep and unmoving, not part of the familiar anymore but of dark, secret pieces of the night. *Now,* Mattie told herself. *You have to do it* now.

Grabbing hold of the banister, she started down the stairs. Her throat felt tight and dry but she couldn't swallow. She was conscious of her accelerated heartbeat, a wild pounding that sounded loud enough to wake the dead.

The stairs creaked and Mattie froze, straining to hear someone else out there in the darkness. A few seconds passed, and the silence only deepened. Mattie descended softly, furtively, testing each step before she put her full weight on it. Her palms were slick with sweat now. Pausing for a second, she tightened her grip on the gun.

Mattie screamed soundlessly as the hand snaked out of the darkness and closed around her ankle, jerking her off balance. Her head smashed against the stairwell. Gasping for breath, she kicked out, trying to break free.

A flash of pure, numbing pain shot through her leg as it crashed against the oak balusters. She twisted her body and swung the heavy automatic around, her trembling hand trying to level it at the moving darkness below the stairs.

She heard a whispery rush of breath. Soft, broken laughter. A second hand closed over the first and yanking hard, jerked her off her feet. Mattie's scream filled the night as she tripped, spun wildly around and hurtled down the stairs.

She heard the laughter again. Then there was nothing but the pain and the soft, easy darkness.

123

Time stopped for a while like a small, sweet foretaste of death. The pain was constant, rising, ebbing, rising again. The darkness began to dissolve, the black slowly being eaten away by soft, pulsing color. She heard a voice, lost it, then heard it again.

The voice sounded distant and muffled, like a bad connection on a call to a different time zone. Mattie slowly became aware of a steady, throbbing pain at the back of her skull, the warm, coppery smell of blood and something cold and wet draped across her forehead. She groaned and blinked her eyes, her gaze finally focusing on the worried face of Sergeant Al Kiefer. Peering down at her he smiled tightly and said, "How are you feeling?"

"All right . . . I think," she muttered. "Nothing's broken but it all hurts like hell." She tried to sit up, but a flash of pain and a sudden feeling of dizziness forced her head back down. She realized she was still on the stairs where she'd fallen. They probably hadn't wanted to move her until they knew the extent of her injuries. The house was now ablaze with light and through the curtained front windows she saw the rotating red beacons of patrol cars strobing the night with bright, angry color. There were two uniformed officers standing by the door and crouched alongside Kiefer was a freckle-faced paramedic with intense blue eyes.

"Do you know who you are and where you are?" he asked her.

Mattie nodded then winced. Nodding, she decided, wasn't such a hot idea. "I'm Mattie Ann Shayne," she said quietly. "And I'm home."

"Would you like to be taken to the emergency room?"

"No, thank you." She grinned weakly and pushed herself upright again, riding out the pain this time. She squeezed her eyes shut and after a moment the dizziness passed. Mattie took a deep breath, opened her eyes and smiled at Kiefer. "Maybe now I can get some time off work."

"A head injury is nothing to joke about," the paramedic

124

said. He sounded solemn and stern, as though he were trying to compensate for looking young enough to be one of Mattie's students. "Take these," he said handing her some pills in a paper packet and a plastic tumbler of water. Mattie shook two of the tiny white tablets into her palm. They tasted the way pills always do but the water tasted wonderful.

"Keep that cold compress on your head," he continued. "And make an appointment to see your own doctor as soon as you can. If the headache persists or if you have any vision problems or attacks of vertigo, have someone drive you to the emergency room. All right?"

"All right," she replied meekly. It was her experience that if you agreed with medical people they usually stopped staring at you and went away. The young paramedic eyed her suspiciously for a few more seconds, then rose abruptly, nodded good night and stalked out the door.

Kiefer sighed and sat down on the steps next to Mattie. He took out his cigarettes, looked at her and stuffed them back in his jacket pocket. "Did you see who it was?" he asked her.

"No. Too dark. I guess you didn't catch him then?"

Kiefer shook his head. "Whoever it was was already gone when the first patrol car got here. Your neighbors, the Olsons, called nine-one-one when they heard you scream.

"I'm here because I happened to catch the call on the radio and I recognized the address. I thought I'd better see what was going down."

"I wonder if Ryder heard the call." As soon as Mattie said it she realized it was dumb. But it was too late to take it back.

"Ryder?" Kiefer repeated. "I doubt it. If he has any sense at all he's home sleeping." He looked past her, studying the brightly lit living room for a moment before shifting his gaze back to Mattie. "What exactly happened here?" he asked softly.

"I woke up and heard someone moving around down here." She decided not to mention the dream. It would sound weird no matter how she told it and it would only make things confusing.

"I have a gun," she continued. "I got it out of the nightstand where I keep it and and started to sneak downstairs. I was near the bottom when someone reached through the stair rails, grabbed my ankle and yanked me off balance. I tried to fight back . . . but there was nothing I could do."

Kiefer nodded. "Lieutenant Ryder told me about the gun. We found it on the floor in the hall. I could have it dusted for prints, but I doubt we'd find anything but yours. Why don't you let me take it anyway. There's always a *possibility* the intruder handled it. Maybe we'll get lucky."

"All right," Mattie said. "It wasn't much use to me anyway."

"I'd like to make sure it wasn't anything more than just breaking and entering." He stood up and held out his hand to her. "Do you think you can manage a quick tour of the premises? We should check to see what's missing, but if you're not up to it we can always wait until tomorrow."

"I'm all right," Mattie insisted. She wrapped her fingers around Kiefer's skinny arm and slowly pulled herself upright. There was a little pain, a touch of dizziness, but she rode it out. Leaning against Kiefer she just stood there for a moment enjoying the feeling of being up on her two feet again. Her head still hurt and she was slightly hung over. She'd been knocked out and probably robbed, all in the middle of a murder investigation. Her life, she decided, was turning into a bad Raymond Chandler pastiche.

"Let's inspect the ruins," she said with a weak smile. With Kiefer holding her arm they made a slow circuit of the living room and dining room. To Mattie's surprise the television and stereo were in their usual places. The thin layer of dust on top of the speakers was undisturbed; it looked as though her burglar wasn't interested in the usual stuff. Mattie's silver service, inherited from her grandmother, was also intact. It was beginning to look as though nothing had been taken until they reached the kitchen.

"My bag," Mattie groaned. "Money, checkbook, credit

cards and keys, it was all in there.'' It was gone from its regular spot on the little stool beside the counter. She clearly remembered putting it there when she came home. Now she'd have to go through the hassle of canceling all her charge cards and informing the bank about the missing checks. Luckily she had a duplicate set of keys, but now she'd have to have all the locks changed. For the first time she felt a sense of violation. It scared her but more than that it made her angry. No one had a right to come into *her* house, to put their grubby hands on *her* things.

Sagging against Kiefer's shoulder, she slowly surveyed the rest of the kitchen.

"We found where he gained entry.'' He led Mattie over to the kitchen door and pointed to a missing pane of glass positioned directly above the lock. "He covered it with masking tape, broke the glass and then took the pieces out. After that all he had to do was reach inside and unlock the door.'' He studied the point of entry for a few more seconds, then took out his Larks and lit one.

"It's a very neat job,'' he said exhaling smoke. "Probably the work of a professional. The only strange thing about it is how little he took.''

"Maybe he's just fussy,'' Mattie said bitterly. "Do you think it might have something to do with the murder investigation?''

Kiefer hesitated. "I honestly don't know,'' he said finally. "It's a real possibility. But there's also been a number of burglary assaults in this neighborhood. Most of the victims have been women who live alone.''

"That's all I needed to hear.''

"It wouldn't do any good for me to lie to you,'' Kiefer said gently. "This is serious, what happened here tonight. We'll do everything we can to try and find the person responsible. Meanwhile, I'm going to arrange for a policewoman to spend the rest of the night. I'll have a friend of mine come over early tomorrow to replace that broken glass and change the locks for you.''

"I don't know what to say You've been . . . "

"Don't say anything. Just get some rest."

She loaned heavily against Kiefer as he led her back toward the stairs. She suddenly felt incredibly tired, as though sleep were something she hadn't experienced in a long, long time.

16

In the morning Lieutenant Ryder appeared on Mattie's door-step, his bulky figure backlit by bright autumn sunlight and his big hands carefully folded around a dozen tissue-wrapped roses.

"How's the invalid?" he asked. His tone was light but the concern was there in his voice. And his troubled blue eyes studied her guardedly, as though he were afraid of what he might see.

"The invalid is fine," she assured him. "My head hardly hurts at all except when I move too fast." She smiled and nodded at the roses. "Are those for me? You'd better say *yes*."

"Absolutely." Ryder hurriedly offered them, the tissue paper making crinkling noises as the flowers exchanged hands. Mattie sniffed their sweet, strong fragrance, her mouth turning up in a crooked grin. The roses were beautiful, all deep, vibrant red long-stems that were just beginning to bud. It had been years since a man, or anyone else for that matter, had brought her flowers. Peter had courted her with books and records, gift certificates, *practical* things. But never flowers. She peered at Ryder over the top of the bouquet. He was watching her expectantly, waiting to see how she'd react.

"They're beautiful," she said softly. "The nicest present anyone's given me in a long time."

"Honestly?" He jammed his hands in his pockets and shifted his stance as though he didn't quiet know how to deal with her gratitude. He managed a smile though, hesitant at first but slowly widening.

"They're wonderful," Mattie assured him. "And that's the truth. I wouldn't lie. At least not to a policeman." With her free hand she reached out and tugged at the sleeve of his jacket, easing him over the threshold like a giant pull toy. "Come back to the kitchen," she insisted "We'll put these in water and then have some coffee."

Seated around the big oak table, they sipped coffee while Ryder brought her up to date on last night's break-in. He was embarrassed to admit that the Burglary Division hadn't made any progress on the case. There were no leads, he reminded her, no witnesses. Nothing for the police to go on. Unless they got lucky, the burglary, like a good many others, would probably remain unsolved.

Mattie wasn't exactly thrilled with the news. But with a murderer still on the loose, a simple break-in, even one involving *her*, suddenly didn't seem all that important. At least Ryder had been honest with her. She also sensed that his interest was *personal*, involving more genuine concern than a cop dealing with just another crime.

When she asked Ryder if he thought that the incident might be connected to the murder investigation, his reaction was the same as Kiefer's; he didn't know.

Ryder drained his coffee cup and then ground out the stub of his cigarette in a lopsided green ceramic ashtray, a gift from one of Mattie's students a few years back. She realized that that was only the second cigarette he'd had since he'd arrived. Was he cutting back on account of her invalid status? Whatever the reason, she was glad to see it happening.

"You have any plans for today?"

"Not really," she said. "I'm not going to hang around the house, though. This weather's too good to waste."

"You feel like helping me out some more? I'd like to talk to Ariana Kendrick again. But only if you feel up to it."

"I'm fine," she insisted. She parted her dark blond hair and gently probed the tender spot at the back of her head. "At least the swelling's gone down. Last night I had a goose egg the size of Plymouth Rock."

130

"It's barely noticeable," Ryder said grinning. "In fact, you look so presentable that I'm going to take you to lunch after we're done. Someplace really nice."

"You're forgetting something."

"What?"

"It's my turn to buy. *I* get to pick the place."

Ryder laughed, got up and helped her to clear the table. She watched out of the corner of her eye as he rinsed the cups and saucers in the sink and then set them to dry on the drain board.

Mattie decided she liked Ryder. She found him attractive and interesting, even though he was at least fifteen years older than she was. But then she'd always been attracted to older men. It had nothing to do with a father fixation. She just found them for the most part more comfortable to be around, more at peace with themselves. They were old enough to know that they couldn't change or save the world all on their own. The smarter ones had come to realize that there was only one way to do it. One day, one person, one moment at a time.

"There's one, short stop I want to make after Kendricks'," he said wiping his hand on the dish towel. "I want to try Charlie Lentz's place again, poke around a little, try and get a line on him."

Mattie frowned. "I thought you had his apartment staked out." She savored the last two words, enjoying the way they rolled off her tongue. They came out soft but clipped, just like Jack Webb on "Dragnet."

"I did and now I don't," Ryder said glumly. "We're short of men right now and I couldn't get anyone to continue the surveillance after midnight. But that's police work." He sighed and shook his head. "If it isn't enough officers to go around then it's the bureaucracy. And if it isn't the bureaucracy it's the paperwork."

"Sometimes," he said with a faint smile, "I wonder how we ever find the time to arrest anybody."

131

17

Ariana Kendrick ushered them into the over-furnished living room just as she'd done two nights before. There was no fire burning in the grate this time. The whole house seemed colder, Mattie noticed, more like a shrine than a place for the living. A thin layer of dust had begun to settle on all the polished oak, muting the reflected shine of the soft morning sunlight. The small, subtle changes reminded Mattie of Charlie Lentz's cramped, dingy apartment. It wasn't in Kenwood and it didn't cost a fraction as much, but now the two places seemed to share a small, sad camaraderie.

"I think I know why you're here," Ariana signed.

Mattie voiced it for Ryder, who nodded but didn't say anything. Taking his notebook out, he smoothed back a fresh page with his thumb.

Ariana shifted around in the deep leather chair, crossed her legs and tugged at the skirt of her gray jersey dress. Finally she took a deep breath. "I lied about what happened the other night," she signed. "Paul and I weren't here the whole time. But then you probably already know that."

Ryder merely nodded again. He was smiling slightly, waiting now for her to fill in the silence with her hands and Mattie's voice.

"We left here around five," Ariana continued. "We took my car and drove downtown for drinks and dinner at the New French Café. There was a long wait for a table . . . we had quite a lot to drink. Paul got in an argument with someone at the bar, a brawl broke out . . . very violent, ugly. I was angry with Paul. He gets like that when he drinks. So I took off and left him there."

"What time would that be?"

She hesitated. "A quarter after six," she signed. "Maybe six-thirty. I drove around for a while, had dinner out by Southdale and then came home. Paul was waiting for me when I got here."

"Why did you lie about it?" Ryder asked softly. "For Linstrum? Is he that important to you?"

Ariana shook her head. "I lied for Paul, yes, but also for his son. Paul is involved in a custody battle with his former wife, who lives down in Iowa, where he's from originally. Paul has a history of DWIs and bar fights, but he's slowly straightening himself out, learning to get it together. Sometimes the pressure's just too much for him. If his ex-wife ever found out about the other night it would really screw up his chances. He's not even looking for shared custody. He just wants to spend some time with the boy."

Ryder closed his notebook and slipped it back in his pocket. "If this all checks out," he said, "I don't think either of you will have to worry about being suspects anymore. I wish you would have told me all this before. It would have saved the department a lot of money and man hours."

"I'm sorry," Ariana signed. She looked as though she honestly was. "Are there any new leads, Lieutenant? Are you going to arrest someone soon?"

"I need to talk to your brother. You know where I can find him?"

"Charlie?" She shook her head. "I haven't seen him in months. We never were that close. You think he might have something to do with Noah's death?" She frowned, the lines around her mouth deepening almost like folds in the skin. Mattie realized she looked older, less pretty but infinitely stronger.

"I just want to talk with him," Ryder said. "I have a feeling he has quite a lot to tell me."

The Casa Loma Gardens looked a little better by bright

sunlight, but the overall effect was still one of slow, steady decay. The cracked, flaking stucco and rust-pitted wrought iron remained unchanged, though, Mattie noticed, the lawn was freshly mown and had been raked clear of yesterday's litter and leaves. Also, the second-story front windows had been washed, the glass sparkling. She remembered the Vietnamese family, the polished banister and the spotless halls. Maybe there was hope for the building yet.

The entryway door was unlocked as before, but this time the halls were quiet, with no snatches of conversation drifting from the apartments to fill the silence. The building was probably empty. It was too nice a day for anyone to stay inside. Ryder took the stairs more slowly this time. He hadn't had a cigarette since they'd left the house, but his breathing was still raspy and strained, the sound of it echoing down the stairwell in counterpoint to their muffled footsteps.

When they reached the top landing, Ryder leaned against the wall and took a deep, steadying breath. "I think I'll pass on the marathon this year," he said with a feeble grin. Mattie squeezed his arm affectionately as he straightened up and nodded at the apartment door. "Let's see if our wandering boy has come home."

He knocked and rang the bell but there was no response. Mattie noticed that the lock was still open and that the door stood slightly ajar. Ryder pressed his palm against the flaking, green metal and the door swung open with a whispery rush of air. A few steps into the tiny foyer, Ryder stopped abruptly and Mattie peered over his shoulder.

"Jesus," she said in a choked whisper.

It looked like Charlie Lentz was home after all. Supported by a thick length of rope around his neck, his bloated body dangled beneath the heavy brass light fixture. His broad face was mottled with dusty color. His tongue protruded, thick and swollen, and his sad, dark eyes seemed to be staring down at them with a look of infinite reproach. There were purplish bruises ringing his neck where the rope had cut deep and Mattie

135

noticed that his glasses had fallen to the dusty floor, landing a few inches away from the overturned kitchen chair.

The air in the room was thick and motionless, heavy with the smells of death. But something, maybe their own movements, set the corpse swaying gently in a grisly parody of animation. Mattie felt her stomach kick, bile rising in her throat. She took a shallow breath and squeezed her eyes shut. But the image of the dead man remained.

"You should cut him down." She knew she said it, but her voice sounded funny, like somebody else's.

"Can't," Ryder said abruptly. "The scene of the crime team has to go over everything first. And it's not like we could help him. Not now anymore." He reached out and took her arm, guiding her out of the apartment. Mattie stumbled over the threshold and Ryder caught her, wrapping his arm around her waist. She leaned against him for support, smelling the mixed scents of tobacco and cologne, feeling the rough texture of tweed along her cheek.

"You gonna be okay?" he asked softly.

Mattie gulped and nodded. "He killed himself. What a horrible way to die."

"It looks like suicide," Ryder admitted. "But we can't be sure yet, not until there's been a full investigation."

Mattie took a deep, slow breath and then let it out. Her stomach was still knotted up but she was beginning to feel a little better. "He murdered Kendrick," she said quietly. "And then when he couldn't live with it, he killed himself."

Ryder nodded thoughtfully. "If we can get some evidence, something that ties it all together, we'll be able to close the case. But there's no point in even thinking about it until we're sure it's suicide. I have to go back inside and call it in," he said looking directly at Mattie. "You gonna be all right?"

"I'll be fine," she insisted.

"Good. But I'm still sending you home in the first patrol car that makes the scene."

Mattie opened her mouth to protest but she couldn't get the

136

words to come out. Home, she suddenly decided, was exactly where she wanted to be.

18

Monday brought a return to normalcy and the commonplace but comforting routine of work. For once, Mattie didn't even mind getting up early, her least favorite part of her job. In fact, she'd awakened a half hour before the alarm was due to go off. Unable to go back to sleep, she'd just lain there, staring up at the ceiling, bleary eyes tracking the network of cracks on the powder blue paint.

She spent part of the morning on paperwork and part of it with her students, losing herself for an hour or two in American History—the causes of the Civil War—and Literature—*Life on the Mississippi*. She'd forgotten how fresh and funny Twain could be. She thought about the murder case and Charlie Lentz's grim demise, but only for brief, scattered moments. The start of the workweek had somehow distanced her from the deaths and everything that surrounded them. The only exception was Ryder. She thought about him a lot. But in a way that had nothing to do with the investigation.

At lunchtime she went to a nearby McDonald's. It was crowded, as usual, but it was also fast and cheap, two prerequisites for a teacher with a busy schedule and another mortgage payment looming large on the horizon. After a short wait in line, Mattie carried away her Chicken McNuggets, fries and coffee and headed for an empty window table.

"Pretty lady." She stopped abruptly at the sound of the familiar voice. Turning, she saw Neil Travers, his long, lanky frame squeezed in behind a table for two. He tipped his weather-stained Stetson back and smiled up at her. "Join me," he invited. "It's no fun eating alone."

She hesitated for a second. She *liked* eating alone, but she realized that there wasn't any polite way to refuse. With a forced smile, she set her tray on the table while Travers cleared a bigger space for her, brushing the lunchtime litter of paper and Styrofoam to his side of the Formica square. Mattie noticed he had a kid's Happy Meal box and next to the brightly colored container there was a miniature orange plastic car that came with the food inside.

Travers caught her eyeing it and Mattie smiled in spite of herself. "Do you actually order that for yourself?" she asked.

The big, rough-hewn artist nodded solemnly. "Get one every time I come here," he said grinning. He picked up the toy car and spun the wheels with a flick of his callused finger. "I send them to my sister's boy back east. Benjie's just four and loves this kind of stuff."

"That's very thoughtful," Mattie said.

She ripped the top off the little container of sweet-and-sour sauce and started to work on her McNuggets.

"How's the investigation going?" Travers asked.

She held up her hand, chewed some more and then swallowed. "Didn't you see it on the news? Kendrick's brother-in-law killed himself. Lieutenant Ryder and I found the body." She dabbed at her mouth with a paper napkin. "It's not," she said firmly, "an experience I'm anxious to repeat."

Travers frowned. "It's definitely suicide then?"

"Well," Mattie hesitated. "They still haven't made it official, but it certainly looks that way. The media's calling it an *apparent* suicide for the time being."

"Flannelmouths," Travers muttered, rubbing his angular jaw. "That's what all those newspeople are. Plenty of talk but no brains."

Mattie wanted to protest, but she didn't. She had a feeling that no matter what she said, it wouldn't change Travers's mind. "Flannelmouths," she repeated instead. "I don't believe I've ever heard that expression before."

"Probably not. It's old cowboy slang. They had different

140

words for just about everything." He leaned forward, a slow, thoughtful smile softening the hard lines of his face. "Neckerchiefs were called *wipes*," he muttered, "ranch foremen were *high salties* or *top screws* and when a cowboy fell in love it was called *calico fever*." Travers sighed. "Colorful stuff, but you don't hear it much anymore."

"That's too bad," Mattie said. "I kind of like it. Appropriate and funny at the same time. I suppose it was bound to die out. Most people listen more to their TVs than to each other. I'm surprised we don't already talk alike."

Travers nodded as he drained the last of his Coke. "Got to get going," he said rising. "Now don't you forget about my show, pretty lady. I'll make sure ya get an invitation."

"Great," she muttered to his retreating back. She wasn't sure anymore if she really wanted to go. But she'd promised and it looked now as though Travers was counting on her coming.

Ariana Kendrick was sitting on Mattie's front steps when she pulled into the driveway that evening. In the gathering dusk, the younger woman cut a striking but somber figure. She was dressed all in black, silk pants and a matching sheath top, high-heeled boots and a scarf wrapped loosely around her neck.

It *was* mourning garb, Mattie decided, but definitely more New Wave than traditional. At least Ariana had the looks to carry it off. She watched Mattie over the glowing tip of a cigarette. As Mattie neared the steps, Ariana rose gracefully, tossed the cigarette on the sidewalk and ground it out under her heel.

The deaf woman smiled hesitantly. "I was about to give up on you," she signed. "I've been waiting awhile." She drew her index finger up along her left arm and then tapped her wrist, indicating an imaginary watch.

Bewildered by it all, Mattie made the sign for sorry. "I didn't know you were coming." Like Travers earlier today, the people in the investigation seemed somehow destined to reappear in Mattie's life, like characters in a play who refuse to leave the stage after the final curtain. Mattie sighed and gestured toward the door. "Come on in," she signed. "We'll be more comfortable inside."

Ariana shook her head. "I just wanted to ask you something. A favor." Her hawkish face momentarily lost its composure; she looked uncertain, almost embarrassed. "Noah's funeral is this Thursday afternoon," she signed nervously. "I was wondering if you would come and interpret the services. It won't take very long and it would mean a lot to me."

"Yes, of course," Mattie signed. It would probably involve taking some time off work but she could arrange that. She was touched that Ariana had thought of her. She realized that, considering her brief involvement in their lives, the gesture was somehow strangely appropriate.

Ariana signed her thanks, then took a folded square of paper out of her bag and handed it to Mattie. "The information is all there," she signed. It was getting harder to read her hands in the fading light. If they were going to continue the conversation much longer they'd have to move inside.

The deaf woman smiled at her. "You never thought I did it, did you?"

"No, I never did," Mattie signed. She hesitated, then added, "I'm sorry about your brother."

Ariana shook her head. "Poor Charlie . . . Poor Noah. Charlie and I were close once, when we were kids. Back in the days when we were a real family. He used to lie in the grass and stare up at the clouds dreaming all his big dreams. But none of them ever came true."

"I wonder why?"

"He never understood how to play the *game*. Life or anything else. Whenever they chose up teams, Charlie was always left on the sidelines, standing alone."

"I'd like to come to his funeral," Mattie signed impulsively.

"We'll probably be the only ones there."

"That's all right."

"I guess he did burn down the cabin, but I still have trouble believing he killed Noah." She signed and shook her head again. "I'd better get going. I have to make arrangements for Charlie's funeral now. I'll let you know when it is."

Ariana squeezed Mattie's arm, nodded and turned away. Mattie watched as she moved down the sidewalk, slim, graceful and elegant, her dark hair ruffled by the evening breeze. The sound of her boot heels gradually faded away, leaving Mattie alone in the gathering darkness.

19

Later that evening, when Mattie was lingering over a second cup of coffee, she started to see it. Everything that she hadn't seen before.

She hadn't been thinking about anything in particular, certainly not the murder investigation. But suddenly an image formed in her mind, random bits of information, words and actions that all connected. The picture she'd come up with was like one of those drawings in a kid's *Rainy Day Fun Book*, the kind where you have to draw the lines between the scattered dots to complete the picture.

The image in Mattie's mind wasn't nearly so pleasant. All the dots were linked together with blood instead of crayon and the picture was one of relentless evil, greed and sudden death.

She stared silently at her empty cup for a few seconds, then stood up and carried it to the sink. "House burned down . . . no iron man there," she said softly. She knew what Kendrick's dying words meant now. It was the only explanation that fit. After all these years of working with the deaf, she should have seen it long before this. Sign language was dominated by visual images, pictures made by hand. And that's what it was. Kendrick had given them two related word-pictures that not only told who killed him but also why.

None of it meant anything, though. Not unless she could get some proof. She glanced at the clock radio on the counter. It was only twenty past seven. The Walker Library was open late this evening. They'd probably have what she needed or at least they'd be able to tell her where to find it.

Mattie hesitated, peering out the kitchen window at the

darkness. The quiet, black night seemed almost to be waiting for her, *daring* her to come out and take just one single step away from her door.

She laughed softly and shook her head. She'd always had too damned much imagination. The murderer had tried to kill her once. She was sure of that now. But the "job" had been left unfinished. Too risky perhaps? Or maybe it was simply no longer necessary? Anyway, that time had come and gone. She'd been lying helpless at the bottom of the steps. It would have only taken a matter of seconds for those quick, strong hands to close around her neck, to choke away the rest of her life with one slow, tightening squeeze.

But it didn't happen, she reminded herself. And it wasn't likely now that it ever would.

She turned away from the window, walked quickly to the front of the house and took her trench coat out of the hall closet. Slipping it on, she looked out again, her eyes slowly sweeping the dark, quiet street. Her hand trembled slightly as it closed on the knob of the door, flicking open the new dead bolt, she stepped outside and quickly locked the door behind her.

The library was only a few blocks away, but Mattie took her car anyway. Parking it in the brightly lit lot behind the Walker Branch, she hurried inside and descended the staircase to the main level two stories below ground.

It took only five minutes to find what she was looking for. It wasn't *proof* yet but she had the books where she was sure proof could be found. She checked out two of them, and cradling the heavy volumes in the crook of her arm, she hurried back up the stairs, out into the crisp, windless night and then home again.

Safely back inside the house, Mattie rechecked the doors and windows making sure they were all locked. She poured herself a glass of wine, picked up the library books from the hall table and went into the living room. Settling into the padded platform rocker, she began to read.

146

A half hour later she found what she was looking for. It still wasn't *real* proof, but it was close enough. She understood Noah Kendrick's dying words now. She knew why he'd been murdered. Once she told Ryder, he'd reopen the investigation. He'd *have* to, because the real murderer was still out there, free and clear, maybe even waiting, patiently, to take another life.

Mattie drained her wineglass, set it down and walked out to the hall. She'd call Ryder now, talk to either him or Kiefer. Get it done, get it *over* with. She lifted the receiver and put it to her ear as her finger began to punch out the number. Suddenly she stopped.

The line was dead.

"Hello, pretty lady."

Mattie forced herself to turn around as Neil Travers emerged from the shadowed corner of the stairwell. His bare feet made a soft, whispery sound on the hardwood floor. In his gnarled hand he held a long-barreled revolver, the gun steady and unwavering, like something carved out of stone.

"What are you doing here?" she demanded. "Put that away. This is *crazy*. I never did anything to you." Her voice sounded shrill in the narrow confines of the hallway. Her throat felt tight and dry. She'd had trouble getting the words out.

Travers merely smiled. "Nice try, but it's not going to buy you anything." He sounded almost regretful. "I followed you home from the library tonight. I know what books you checked out: Ramon Adams's *The Old-Time Cowhand* and Watts's *A Dictionary of the Old West*. You found it, didn't you? You know what 'iron man' means?"

Mattie nodded. There was no point in lying now. It might make him angry and she didn't want that. Not yet.

"It was you all the time," she said. "Wasn't it?"

"I've been watching you ever since we took care of Kendrick. The radio in my truck can pick up the police band. You never *saw* me but I was there. In the emergency waiting room, outside Kendrick's house, in the alley back of here the next

147

day.'' He paused, a slow, ugly grin splitting his face. ''I feel like we're *almost* friends. It's a shame that I have to kill you.''

''How did you get in here?''

''Through the basement window. It was a tight squeeze, but I made it.'' He waved the gun at her, the long barrel winking in the light. ''We're wasting time,'' he muttered. ''Let's move out to the kitchen. There's someone else who wants to see you.''

Meredith, the pudgy gallery owner, was perched on the edge of the kitchen table. He looked nervous and uncertain. Mattie noticed that his plump hands were trembling and that he was wearing the same yellow sweater that he'd had on that day at the gallery. Tapping the linoleum with the toe of his scuffed loafer, he leaned forward, his gaze restlessly shifting from Mattie to Travers and then back again as he waited to see one of them speak.

''How'd ya figure it out?'' Travers asked softly.

Mattie shrugged. ''It was simple once you understood Kendrick's message. You gave me a big clue yourself when you told me about cowboy slang.'' She forced herself to relax. She had to draw this out for as long as she could. It was hard to believe that she was here in her own kitchen making polite conversation with a couple of murderers. The scent of warming coffee filled the air, adding an absurd note of domestic tranquility to the scene. Mattie realized that she'd forgotten to turn the machine off before she'd gone out. It had a tendency to overheat if left on for too long. But right now that was the least of her worries.

''I got the *iron man* part of it first,'' Mattie continued. ''You said in the Old West they had different names for just about everything. One of the Russells at the gallery depicted an elderly cowhand wielding a branding *iron*. According to the Adam's book on cowboy lore, the hand with that job was often called the *iron man*. I think that was the title of the Russell painting too.''

Travers smiled. ''It was. We even had it listed in the pro-

148

gram. That's why I had to break in here the other night. You picked up a program at the gallery but there wasn't anything I could do about it then. Thanks for leaving it in your bag; it made it easier to find.''

"You want to hear the rest of it?" she said quickly. Travers was beginning to look bored. Not a healthy sign, especially where her health was concerned. "I worked it out," she rattled on. "But it wasn't easy."

The big artist nodded abruptly. "Tell me about it. But make it short. The clock's running out."

She took a deep breath, trying not to think about what he'd just said. "The *house burned down* part was harder," Mattie went on. "Everyone thought it meant the Kendricks' cabin up north. But if he meant cabin, he would have finger-spelled *cabin*, not house. Lieutenant Ryder told me that among Kendrick's papers was an article he was writing about prairie fires and that a large part of it concerned a ranch *house* that burned down in nineteen ten. Apart from the cabin, it was the only other fire that fit."

"The old Dougherty spread," Travers interrupted. "To establish the provenance, the source of these long-lost Russells, old Todd here worked out a deal with this Montana rancher, who was supposed to say he found them in the attic."

"Now *that's* original," Mattie said.

"Shut up," Travers snapped. The gun rose slightly and Mattie went dead still. For a moment the only sound was the whispery rush of breathing. Mattie wanted to squeeze her eyes shut, but she couldn't do it.

Travers relaxed, leaning back against the kitchen door. "Anyway," he continued. "Neither the current owner of the ranch or my genius associate here," he paused and nodded at Meredith, "knew that the place had burned down in nineteen ten and was rebuilt the following year. The problem was that the goddamned paintings *predated* the fire, so that logically they would have been destroyed along with everything else." Travers sighed. "When Kendrick saw that note about the

149

Dougherty Ranch in the program, he knew something wasn't right."

"That's the way I figured it," Mattie admitted. "I didn't have it all doped out. Just enough to see the connection."

"You're smart," he said grinning at her. "Maybe I should have partnered up with you instead of him." They both glanced over at Meredith. The chunky deaf man looked uncomfortably aware that he was the topic of conversation. He probably hadn't wanted to be here in the first place. Travers must have forced him to come along.

"Who painted the forgeries?" she asked hurriedly.

Travers tapped his chest with a calloused finger. "Yours truly," he said. His voice had taken on an added warmth; she'd obviously hit on his favorite topic of conversation. "I spent years on those beauties," he elaborated. "Found some old canvases, the work of a third-rate western painter from the same period as Russell. That's what gave me the original idea. Slowly, painstakingly, I reworked them into masterpieces that even old Charlie himself wouldn't be able to tell from his own. Fooled one of the top experts in the country," he added smugly. "Then after a quick showing for respectability's sake, the paintings are off to Europe. The sale's already complete and the money, as they say, is in the bank."

"Impressive," Mattie said. She couldn't keep this up much longer. Her gaze wandered for a second, then stopped on the coffee machine beside her on the counter.

She quickly looked the other way. The glass coffee pot was nearly half-full and the handle was angled around in her direction. Travers was on the other side of the narrow kitchen and Meredith off to her left. She just might be able to do it if she timed it right. It was her best, no, her *only*, chance.

"So Kendrick threatened to expose you then?"

Travers nodded curtly. The conversation seemed to be dying.

"So you killed him," Mattie blundered on, "and alibied each other. But what about Charlie Lentz? His death wasn't really a suicide?"

150

"Lentz." Travers repeated the name as though it brought a sour taste to his mouth. "That stumblebum followed Kendrick to the gallery and waited outside. He wanted to hit him up for another loan. Anyway, he saw us take Kendrick out the back door and shove him in my van. He didn't do anything to stop it, but when he read about the murder the next day he made a *very* big mistake." He paused and sighed audibly. "Some people just aren't cut out for blackmail. I put poor Charlie on ice for a while, then arranged for him . . . "

Mattie jerked her head in Meredith's direction. As Travers's eyes followed her gaze, Mattie grabbed the coffee pot and tossed it across the room.

Wood splintered above her head, followed a split second later by the thunderous explosion of the shot. The coffee pot shattered against the far wall, showering Travers with the scalding liquid and broken glass. He screamed and fell to his knees, the big gun skittering out of his hand and down to the worn linoleum.

Mattie dove for it, beating out Meredith by seconds. He scrambled back toward the table as she raised it in her shaking hands. The damn thing weighed a ton, she'd probably wind up shooting herself if she had to use it. Trembling convulsively now, she slowly backstepped to where she could lean against the counter. The damned gun barrel kept dipping and bobbing. Even with two hands she couldn't keep it steady.

Groaning, Travers staggered to his feet. One of his eyes was squeezed shut and his lined face was peppered with little cuts, the tanned flesh glowing in random splotches where the coffee had splattered it. He looked like he was in pain, but more then anything, he looked angry and determined.

"Don't move," Mattie warned him. The ringing in her ears was so loud that she could barely hear herself.

Travers grinned crookedly and took a hesitant step forward. "You're not gonna shoot me," he crooned. "Not you, pretty lady."

Mattie smiled and squeezed the trigger.

151

Again the kitchen filled with thunderous noise, as the heavy gun bucked in her hands. Travers screamed as the force of the shot slammed him against the wall, where he rested for a moment like a tired drunk before sliding slowly down to the floor. His chambray shirt was beginning to soak up the dark, coppery-smelling blood that seeped down from the fleshy part of his shoulder.

His mad eyes gleaming up at her, Travers began to pull himself upright. He gritted his teeth, the muscles of his neck and shoulders were corded and glistened with sweat. He locked one scarred hand over the counter edge and slowly, painfully pulled himself to his feet. Wincing, he rested there for a second, smiled and began to stagger toward Mattie.

"No," she whispered. "No."

When he didn't stop, she slowly raised the gun again and squeezed the trigger. As the sound of the shot faded, Mattie heard the wail of distant sirens.

20

It was nearly morning before it was all over. When the last of the paperwork was completed, Ryder woke Mattie, who'd fallen asleep in his office chair. They walked down from the second-floor headquarters of the Homicide Division and outside, pausing at the top of the Old Courthouse stairs.

Mattie breathed the sweet morning air and smiled. Beside her, Ryder lit a cigarette and squinted up at the sky where soft, warm colors were starting to push the darkness away. He looked at Mattie and lightly touched her arm.

"You want to talk about it?" he asked.

She shook her head. "Not now. I have to think about it. It's not at all like I imagined it would be. I know I *had* to do it, but that doesn't make any difference. The *reality* of taking another person's life. I don't know how to live with that yet."

"Anytime you want to talk about it. I'll be around."

"Thanks," Mattie said softly. "The same goes for me. Anytime you want to talk about your former partner and how he died." She hesitated. "Just let me know."

Ryder nodded. "I'm not ready for that yet. Not for a while."

They walked down the worn stone steps together. Ryder tossed his cigarette away and looked at her again. "I think our relationship is changing," he said quietly.

"You're right, it's changing. But it has been ever since we met. Everything changes, constantly. For good, or worse, for no reason at all. Relationships only stop changing when they're *over*," she said smiling. "Considering we've only known each other a couple of days, I'd say we had a ways to go."

She slipped her arm through Ryder's and together they strode across Courthouse Square to the car.

If you have enjoyed this mystery and would like to
receive details of other Walker mysteries
please write to:

Mystery Editor
Walker and Company
720 Fifth Avenue
New York, New York 10019